MW00737100

BRAZILIAN MOON AND UNRELATED STORIES

Carol Fox

CAROL FOX

Published by Circleville Fox
This book is a work of fiction. Names, characters, businesses, organizations, places, events, and incidents either are the product of the author's imagination or are used fictitiously. Any resemblance to actual persons, living or dead, events, or locales is entirely coincidental.

ISBN 978-0-9970416-2-0

Table of Contents

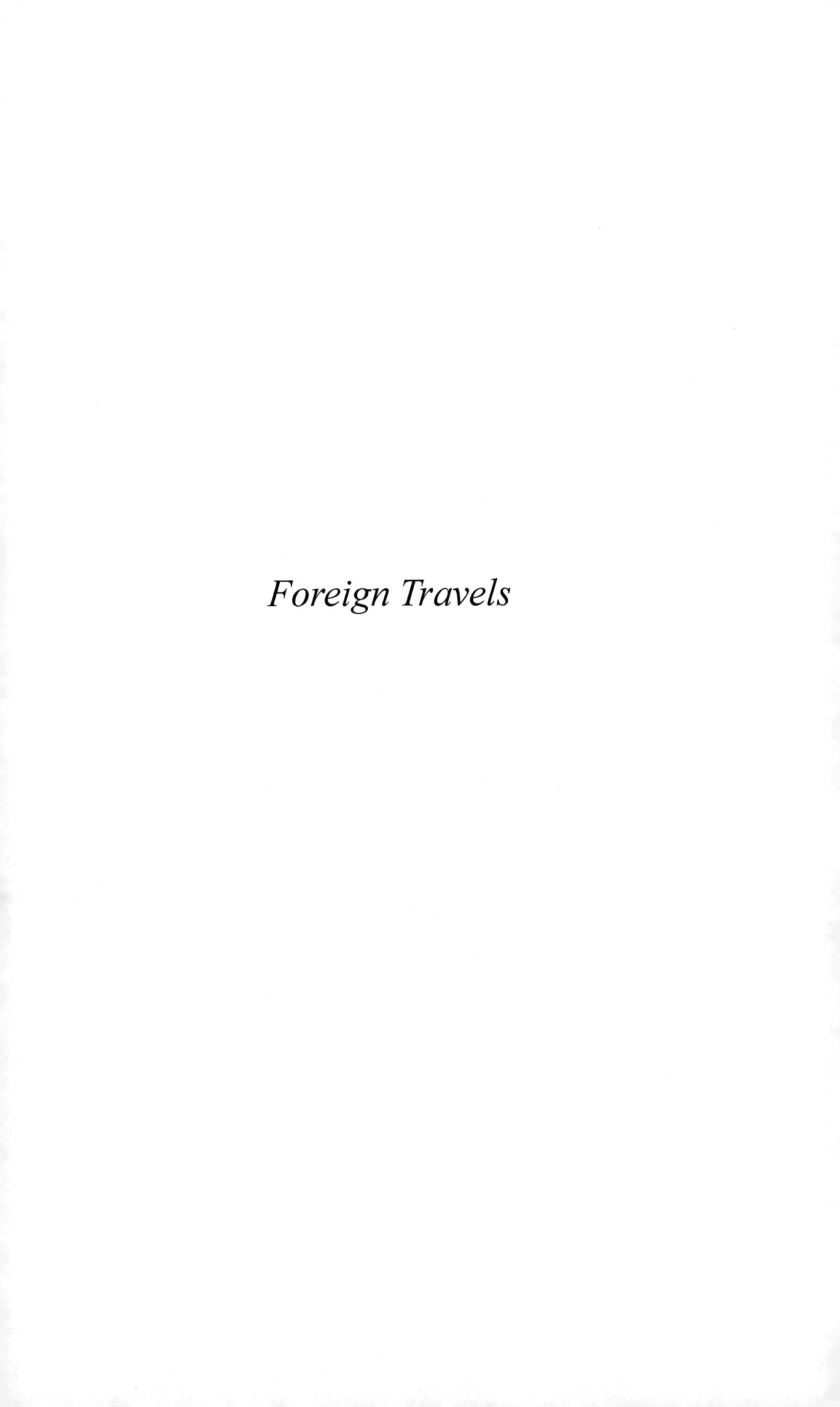

Foreign Travels

María del Perú

In the iron bedstead, Dr. Mendoza lies staring, the right side of his mouth twisted down, arms and legs limp on the worn sheets. A nun enters, moves aside a vase of irises to place a tray on the bedside table, then silently sways out of the room.

When María and her daughter arrive, he strains to speak, but emits only strange burbling noises. He fixes his dark eyes on María, the intensity of his gaze telegraphing his desperation. María freezes until his eyes turn imploringly to his goddaughter. Then she wheels and runs, dragging Teresa by the hand.

That's what she told me, anyway. A year later Dr. Mendoza died, but María had never gone back. She told me about it when I returned to Peru some years later. María had gained weight, but otherwise looked the same, though more prosperous. A flowing, gold-patterned blouse set off her dark brown hair and eyes.

"Mi hermanita," she said, clasping my hand as we sat in the upscale Miraflores restaurant. At the pension she was assured, but here she seemed to feel she should be clearing off the dirty dishes and serving the coffee.

"¿Recuerdes?" she asked.

Yes, I remember.

***

In the damp Limeñan night, we waited in the big black sixties Chevrolet for Dr. Mendoza to retrieve the windshield wipers locked in the trunk. Señora Mendoza sat in the front seat. In the back, María, his assistant, alternately clasped and patted my hand, claiming this visitor from another world as her own. Protestors milled around the entrance to the airport, held in check by teenage soldiers with heavy rifles.

A light drizzle followed us from the airport, smearing the dark streets. "It never rains," Dr. Mendoza said.

Avenida de la Marina, heading east toward the suburb of Miraflores, traversed a dimly lighted industrial district, drab and dirty. Plans had changed, Dr. Mendoza said. The boardinghouse the university had arranged for me was now quarantined because one of the boarders was dying of typhus. Just days before my arrival, the university had assigned me to Dr. Mendoza.

Driving slowly, Dr. Mendoza wandered the dark unmarked streets of Miraflores. As it grew later and later, conversation suddenly ceased. The stern lines of Dr.

Mendoza's face grew sterner.

He consulted his directions one last time, circled back, and as if by intuition stopped before a large house indistinguishable from the others in the sleeping neighborhood. I had a confused impression of light, polished wood floors, a curving staircase, hasty goodbyes, and the big black Chevrolet speeding off into the blackness.

Just five minutes before the 1:00 A.M. curfew, imposed because of terrorist attacks by Sendero Luminoso and Túpac Amaru, Dr. Mendoza reached home, and María had to stay the night with the Mendozas.

***

"Won't you have a coffee?" Dr. Mendoza asked when my class was over. His thin dark hair lay straight against his large head, and he held his broad body erect. His face in repose was solemn and dignified.

María closed up the language lab, her domain, with its large-reel tapes—American equipment from the sixties—checked Dr. Mendoza's schedule for the next day, and watched him lock up the steel classroom door that exited onto the steel walkway.

Irrigation channels ran blue today from the chemistry lab's discharge, a line of color in the powdery bare earth.

In the car, María stared out the passenger window, silent.

"I need to stop at the store. Do you have the time?" Dr. Mendoza asked, turning toward the back seat.

"Certainly," I said.

Light from the open door dimly illuminated open barrels of beans, peas, corn, popcorn, rice, chicken feed, rabbit feed. Dr. Mendoza nodded to María. She filled a scoop with beans, another with rice. The clerk placed a sheet of newspaper on scales behind the wooden counter, measured out half a kilo from the scoop, then folded, turned and refolded the newspaper until it formed a sealed package holding the beans. A ray of sunlight picked up motes swirling above a barrel of corn.

"She didn't have anything at home to feed her children," Dr. Mendoza whispered to me.

* * *

"Oh, yes," María said, "it was so romantic." Her deep brown eyes softened. Her small capable hands rested lightly on the dark wool of her skirt.

We sat on a bench in a park near El Centro, Lima's old town. On the sidewalk waddled a pigeon—big *paloma*, as opposed to little *paloma*, the dove so plaintive in the mornings.

"He still calls once a year or so. I tell him I love him. I tell him I'm waiting for him to return."

A green bus arrives at the bus stop; thick black idling exhaust wafts its way to us as passengers disembark and others patiently wait to board.

After the birth of their eighth daughter, María's husband abandoned her, moved to Venezuela with another woman, fathered six more children.

"If only my son hadn't died."

* * *

Crowds surged in front of the locked gates to the university. On the street in front, large stones blocked the lanes giving access to the university. A line of burning oil, dribbled across the width of the entire street, filled the air with an acrid scent. I saw Dr. Mendoza, in his customary charcoal trousers, dark tie, white shirt, and charcoal sweater, among the crowd gathered in front of the gates, with María by his side.

"The strikers have shut down the university for the day," Dr. Mendoza said. "Let's have a coffee." Dr. Mendoza was a broad man, shorter than I though of average height for Peru, with a dignified bearing. As godfather to one of María's daughters, Teresa, he took his duties seriously, as he did all his responsibilities.

On campus were several one-room places to eat, adobes rising from the dirt. The proprietors were ageless Indian women, their skin adobe colored. Dr. Mendoza knew them all well. This occasional coffee after work was María's only break from her daily, unchanging routine: running the language lab, keeping up with Dr. Mendoza's schedule, returning home to care for her children. But today the little adobes were behind locked gates.

Entering a regular coffee shop in El Centro, with much higher prices, we walked past a wooden case displaying fancy pastries.

"May we have dessert?" María asked, beseeching Dr. Mendoza like a little girl, almost curtsying. Dr. Mendoza beamed with pleasure and told us to order what we liked.

Afterwards, the afternoon stretched before us. We passed through Plaza 2 de Mayo, where I daily changed buses on the way to the university. Like the spokes of a wheel, eight streets entered the circle of the Plaza 2 de Mayo, with cars honking and weaving across traffic at high speeds round and round the circle until they were disgorged onto the proper street. Pedestrians thronged the sidewalks and forced their way through the gauntlet of vendors' carts and deft pickpockets, stepping carefully to avoid stinking pools of rotting garbage. The atmosphere was electric with desperation and danger, awareness the key to survival.

Under a leaden sky, in the district called La Perla, we parked before María's house, a narrow adobe wedged between two others with which it shared walls. A few blocks away, the cold Pacific beat against the Port of Callao. María was almost skipping down the sidewalk.

"Do you like it? It's so small. Do you like it?"

Inside were the youngest two daughters—Lourdes, the one "with problems," and Niki, the baby—and the anciana, a tiny Indian woman with missing teeth who cared for the children while María worked.

"She is my sister," María said, putting her arm around the wrinkled anciana." And this is Señora Margaret Wulferson," she continued, turning to the small anciana.

The old woman had been eating a roll and when María made the introduction, she left crumbs on my cheek where she kissed it. María hastily wiped my cheek off.

The old woman began speaking rapidly to me in heavily accented Spanish. I looked helplessly at María.

"She doesn't speak Spanish," María said to the anciana.

"Oh," she said, brightening, "you speak Quechua," and began to speak rapidly in her own language.

"No, no, inglés," María said.

The old woman looked blank for a moment, then continued to chatter away in heavily accented Spanish. She spent most of her time at María's, taking care of the younger children. Her own last son was cared for by a relative.

A little dog, with funny ears and a tail too long and plumed for her small body, strolled through the living room with great dignity—guardian of a household of eight: María, the six daughters still at home, and the anciana. In the tiny courtyard visible through the living room window, a white duck groomed itself under the lone papaya tree.

"Even counting the duck, we are an all female household," María said, laughing. "The girls found it in the street, but no one in the neighborhood knew where the duck came from, so we kept it. Then she began to lay eggs, big eggs. The girls have them for lunch."

From a small shelf on the opposite wall of the living room, María pulled out all her albums, showing picture after picture of the family. The early photos included a handsome man. The girls gathered round the couch looking with love and admiration at the father who had abandoned them.

***

"Poor María, it's so sad," Dr. Mendoza said as we sat at the back of his classroom, "eight daughters to care for all alone. Such is life."

The Mendozas themselves had had no children. Señora Mendoza had a business downtown designing exclusive clothes, and Dr. Mendoza held a position of importance at the university, but both took very seriously their roles as godparents to one of María's daughters. As an abandoned single mother, María was under their protection.

Sentences in English—exercises—covered the dusty blackboard at the front of the room. Dr. Mendoza's desk, piled with papers to grade, sat at the back. He shook his head gravely.

"Two of her daughters are married. One in Spain—so far away. Six still at home. But what can she do? He left her."

* * *

"Beautiful," María said, using one of her few English words and gesturing out the shabby bus window at the city bordering the cold Pacific, shrouded by the high fog enclosing it. She was taking me on a tour of the old colonial center of Lima.

The elegant plazas connected by grand avenues, the carved wooden balconies overlooking narrow streets—the good bones of the central city, like the high cheekbones in the ruined face of a worn-out courtesan, attested to the former beauty of the city once called the loveliest in South America. Now a dingy pall of soot overlay every surface, garbage lay rotting on the crowded streets, and the perpetual high overcast drained all remaining color from the soot-dimmed buildings. Young, poorly trained soldiers stood at street intersections, holding their rifles carelessly.

In Cafe Haiti near the central post office, María savored her coffee. It cost a fortune in her eyes.

"I don't usually tell anyone, but Teresa got typhoid fever a year after my husband left us. Times were so hard."

"But why not mention it?"

"We didn't have enough to eat. That's why she got sick—no resistance. I couldn't let anyone know. I cared for her day and night, kept her away from the other girls. Gracías a Díos, she survived and none of the other girls got sick."

Buses and cars, mostly American from the fifties and sixties but an occasional brand new Toyota, crowded streets designed for horses and the carriages of the wealthy. Sidewalks, narrowed even more by carts of the street vendors, overflowed with people. But the Haiti was set back from the street, a serene distance from the pulsing, seething humanity.

"How beautiful," María said, glancing around the courtyard of the café. She wore the dark gray skirt she wore most days, and a cream-colored blouse. University faculty and administration, as well as the staff, wore sober and respectable clothes, day after day, for they were dedicated to a higher mission. The Haiti, however, attracted fashionable people with money to lavish. Its prices were equivalent to American ones.

"When the girls were young, it was so hard to feed them, clothe them, educate them. But as each girl graduates from high school, my goal is to pay for one year of secretarial school. Then each can work to pay for any further education. Like Gaby, secretary in the math department and taking courses at the university. And two others married, Cessy in Spain and Luisa here."

Only five more to go, I thought, and sipped my coffee.

* * *

Christmas Eve day, Kennedy Park in downtown Miraflores was crammed with vendors hawking their wares —t-shirts, stuffed animals, trinkets—and the crowds made the sidewalks almost impassable. The expensive Miraflores stores were spilling over with the well dressed wealthy. The beggars, too, were out in great numbers on this day. Impassive women sat on sooty sidewalks with two or three or four small children, the baby in a blanket on the back, the older ones napping on the sidewalk or running around nearby with dirty legs. An Indian woman with five children sat sullen, a torn blanket pulled across her shoulders, holding out her tin cup without acknowledging the coins placed in it. A good-humored man with the stumps of an amputated arm and leg smiled broadly as he held out his cup with his one remaining hand.

By evening the scene was even more frantic: sidewalks solid with people, some lined up to enter stores, others bustling by. From inside the small, beat-up bus full of people clutching packages, I looked at the brightly lit scene outside. Suddenly the inside of the shabby bus taking me to María's seemed cozy and comfortable.

The six daughters still at home, ranging from good-looking to beautiful, crowded around. None spoke English. All had heard María's many stories, but now she introduced us.

"Mar-gar-et," said one, trying out the syllables.

"*Señora* Mar-gar-et," corrected María.

Although María had run the English lab for years, she had never learned more than a few words of English. Yet she showed an amazing ability to communicate. I was sure that if she lived in an English-speaking country, she would rapidly pick up the language.

María passed around the box of chocolates I had brought, carefully supervising her children as each took just one. With so many people, it did not seem as big a box as I had thought. The younger girls very carefully folded up the gold and silver foil wrappers to save.

The closer it grew to midnight, the more excited the girls became. Everyone gathered in a circle on the concrete living room floor, and at the stroke of midnight hugged everyone else.

"Feliz Navidad," the girls repeated many times over.

From María's little hoard, the older girls got a present or two apiece: a t-shirt, a pair of house shoes, a hairbrush. For the two youngest, a little more. Niki, at twelve the baby, leapt up when she unwrapped a plain ball the size of a soccer ball and began to kick it around.

Though María required the girls to open presents in turn, one at a time, still the little ceremony was soon over.

"Feliz Navidad," the girls said once more, sitting suddenly quiet amid the small remains of wrapping paper.

* * *

Tears welled up in María's deep brown eyes as she lay on her side of the bed. I occupied Teresa's place. Gaby had gone out with her boyfriend, a student at the university, and had not come home. That she was staying the night with her leftist boyfriend remained unspoken.

"He's not a Catholic," María said, "and now Gaby says she's a Protestant. What do Protestants believe?"

I searched my memory.

"They believe that one's relationship to God is direct, without an intermediary. Just the person and God."

"I believe that," María said.

Just the morning before, Dr. Mendoza's errands had taken the three of us to Magdalena del Mar, a small suburb on the sea. It was a damp day, with a wind blowing in from the cold gray Pacific. In the distance we could see the Church of the Virgin of Fatima towering above the houses of Magdalena, its steeple shrouded in mist, looking very Eastern and mysterious. Inside were ornate gilt walls, statuary, large murals high up the walls.

María stopped, transfixed by an enormous statue of the Virgin of Fatima, a storey and a half tall.

"She is to be placed on top of the church," Dr. Mendoza said in a hushed tone.

"I have never seen One so huge," María said reverently.

Now, eyes damp with tears, María relaxed on her bed. "Que Dios nos bendiga."

* * *

On a warm summer day (February in Lima), we stopped once again at the little store near the university in this northern part of the city, where Dr. Mendoza and María often shopped. With us today was Dr. Mendoza's young nephew.

The store was cool and dim and inviting, the only light coming from the open front door. Dust motes swirled in a slanting shaft of light illuminating an open barrel of rabbit feed. Next to it stood a barrel of chicken feed, and I thought of the found duck. Once I arrived at María's to find the two youngest girls seated quietly at the dinner table before plates of rice with a large fried egg on top of each, a standard dish in Peru, equivalent to our scrambled eggs and toast. An important gift from the duck, now a valued member of the household.

María gathered up her rice and beans, and I followed her out the door. Dr. Mendoza had finished his shopping first, and we found him across the street buying mangoes, with his nephew beside him. I bought one, too. Here a mango cost nine intis; mangoes from the vendors outside the Wong grocery store in upscale Miraflores sold for thirty-five.

Incongruously, a wide grassy median filled with orange yellow calla lilies separated the two lanes of this out-of-the-way street in a sparsely populated neighborhood, with a small park across the street—such as are mandated by Lima city ordinance to grace the city at intervals, so much parkland per given unit of population. In my wanderings I had often stumbled upon such hidden gems as this little one. Dr. Mendoza's heavy black Chevy was parked next to it.

Dr. Mendoza had bought the mangoes, one for each of us, to eat right now. We re-entered the store to wash them, then crossed the wide median to the big black Chevy. Dr. Mendoza and his nephew sat in front, María and I in back, leaning against the wide upholstered seats.

It was late afternoon and the sun slanted across the green grass and the yellow orange calla lilies. The vendor had packed up his cart and left for the day. Far from the frantic central city, a hush had fallen over the quiet neighborhood.

We sat in the car, loosening the red-blushed peels of the ripe mangoes and savoring the yellow flesh, while rich yellow juice ran between our fingers and dripped on our clothes.

From my purchases I pulled out a roll of toilet paper, and we unwound long strips trying to mop up as we ate, while the sweet juice ran down our arms and fell where it would.

Finally Dr. Mendoza gave up and got out of the car to stand in front where he could lean over and let the juice fall free. His young nephew followed shortly and the two of them stood side by side, dripping and laughing.

María and I remained in the car, staying the flow of sweet mango juice with soggy lengths of toilet paper. I continued sucking on my seed a long time, savoring the sweet tartness, the feathered strands of the mango fibers catching in my teeth.

When Dr. Mendoza and his nephew returned to the car, María began wiping Dr. Mendoza off with toilet paper, clucking and calling him a baby as she scrubbed first at his white shirt, then at his face. The nephew was bragging that his shirt had escaped, but I spotted drops of yellow orange he had missed. In revenge, he gleefully pointed out spots on my blouse. Soon we were all shouting at the splatters of juice on one another. For a time María tried to get away with claiming she was spatter free, but was forced to admit that early on she had wiped off a trailing strain of yellow.

When the last stain had been ridiculed, scrubbed, or abandoned, we sat quietly for a moment, looking out at the yellow light falling softly on the yellow orange flowers, on the yellow mango juice and abandoned peels lying in the grass. From a distance came the faint plaintive call of an unseen dove.

"Someday when you are back in Texas," María said, staring out at the late afternoon light falling gently on the flowers and grass, "you will remember our sitting here, eating mangoes."

* * *

On one of those rare days in winter when the *garua,* the high fog that turned Lima colorless, had lifted, we climbed a spiral iron staircase leading to the top of a large house now divided into apartments. The flat roof of the grand house was open except for a small bedroom and bath and a roofed but otherwise open cooking area off to one side: formerly the maid's quarters, but everyone pretended not to notice. Lima lay quiescent in the gathering dusk.

"It's a good thing we brought no children," María said, glancing at two heavily made-up women. Although dubious, at the last minute she had accepted Angie's invitation.

"This is Victor," Angie said, introducing a small, suave man. "He makes documentaries. And this is Juan."

Juan was an older man, with large features and coarse skin.

"And Fernando, Adelia's brother."

Young and fresh faced, Fernando looked out of place. At six feet, large and lean, he was very tall for a Peruvian. He turned to María.

The persistent overcast hanging over Lima had thinned and the stars shone overhead. A drink in one hand, a cigarette in the other, María spoke earnestly with Fernando, her dark eyes warm and serious. Soon they were dancing.

Moving sinuously to the music, María entered another world, free from all her responsibilities—and from Dr. Mendoza. Dr. Mendoza, who would have fainted to see her, drink in hand, cigarette poised between two fingers.

But now, high up on the rooftop underneath the bright stars, María danced and danced.

***

"Sit down, sit down," María said. She carried a tray with cream and sugar and a pot of coffee, the smooth mild Peruvian coffee.

The two youngest girls were home from school, Gaby back from the university. Teresa, just arrived from work, answered a knock at the door.

"Jose," she exclaimed, escorting him to the dining table. Cessy's husband's brother, he brought pictures of his recent visit to the young couple in Spain.

Jose sat next to María and laid the pictures out like cards. Niki and Lourdes circled in and out in their excitement, while Gaby and Teresa leaned over the table. Jose kept up a running commentary interrupted by exclamations and questions.

The anciana sat on the worn arm of the couch at the farthest edge of the living room, feet swinging above the drab concrete floor, listening to the conversation.

"Look, look," María said, handing me one of the pictures.

I sipped my coffee and looked around. The living room couch and chairs were shabby, the rooms small and few in number for so many people, but the children radiated health and happiness.

"Goodbye, goodbye," called all the girls as Jose took his leave.

"More coffee?" María asked, while emptying the pot into our cups. We drank the last of the mild Peruvian coffee while the girls scattered, some to do homework, others to prepare their clothes for the next day.

"Do you have to go?" María asked as I picked up my backpack. María had taught me to wear it in front, nestling on my breast like an infant in a baby carrier, arms wrapped protectively around it to frustrate pickpockets.

"Why are you in the living room! Carry these dishes to the kitchen," she barked at the tiny wrinkled anciana, using the same abusive tone of command I had heard the last of the oligarchy use to their Indian servants.

"Be careful," María said as I got on the bus, waving

to me as the bus ground gears down the unpaved street, a small sturdy figure motionless in the grey dust under a grey enclosing sky.

***

"Can we go into Los Portales?" María asked Dr. Mendoza as the three of us walked down Abancay Avenue in El Centro—the old Spanish colonial center. We picked our way through jostling crowds and around vendors usurping the grimy sidewalk. Cars screeched around great buses grinding to a halt, and thick poisonous exhaust permeated the air. The buildings on either side of the street were a uniform sooty grey, and the din of the street was unrelenting.

Dr. Mendoza maneuvered me around the bustling crowd, through a stone archway—and into another world.

A man was silently mowing by hand the brilliant green grass of a beautiful garden anchored by four statues of saints, one at each corner. Once a Spanish convent, Los Portales now sequestered small shops down arched walkways radiating from the garden at its center. The quiet and calm of the meditative religious life had been bequeathed to upscale shops and their patrons: windows filled with Maidenform lingerie, color televisions, tape recorders, fashionable clothing.

In the soothing stillness, María tripped along the walks, peeking into every store.

"How much is this one?" María asked, caressing a pale green jogging suit with her strong worn hands.

The shopkeeper named a price equivalent to two months' salary for María.

"It's very nice for sleeping on chill nights," he said,

"but also quite attractive for daytime wear."

"This would be a nice color for Teresa, don't you think?" María said, turning to me and holding the pale green next to the dusky brown skin of her face. Her fingers caressed the fabric she would never touch again.

"I'll be back another time."

"Very good, Señora."

* * *

"María needs to have her iron repaired," Dr. Mendoza said. "Afterwards we can get a coffee—and pie." This was our usual after-work routine: a round of chores, sometimes coffee, before Dr. Mendoza let us off at our respective bus stops, me to the upscale suburb of Miraflores, María to her little house near the Port of Callao with her six daughters waiting.

In a warehouse district in El Centro I had never seen before, jammed with vendors' carts carrying glass cases of hardware or electronics, the sidewalks were so choked the milling people could hardly move.

"Careful," María warned, trying to keep me close. She had taught me to be always alert and aware in the turbulent streets of Lima.

We shoved our way through, wending past cart after cart till we reached a large one, its glassed-in shelves crammed with wires and small parts. Suddenly, men opened heavy clanging doors in the wall behind the cart to reveal a long corridor, at the end of which was a warehouse, and the woman had to roll her cart to one side.

From the top of a huge truck in the street, a man dropped hundred-pound sacks of lentils to other men who loaded them on dollies, rolled them over the curb and then echoing down the long corridor to the warehouse. The labels on the sacks read Moscow, Idaho.

I crossed the street to examine the busy scene from a different perspective. When I returned, María ran to me, frantic.

"Where have you been? I was so worried. Where did you go?"

"I thought she was going to cry when she looked up and couldn't see you," Dr. Mendoza said.

I didn't speak as we walked back to the car with María's iron.

A street person, washing windshields for tips, plied his rag with rapid, exaggerated movements, like a speeded up movie reel. He tossed it spinning high into the air, headed it onto the windshield like a soccer ball, then whizzed it back and forth across the windshield with comically abrupt and jerky strokes. Tossing it, catching it, heading it, whirling it, zipping it back and forth across the car window—in a non-stop routine. People on both sides of the street had stopped to watch, and the two women inside the car were cracking up with laughter.

Dr. Mendoza gazed straight ahead, as though averting his eyes from a disreputable sight, and urged us on. But María gave a quick backwards glance at the show, the corners of her mouth curving upward in a smile.

From the front seat, María turned toward me in back.

"You scared me to death when you disappeared. I was afraid something awful had happened. Don't ever do that again."

"Don't be silly. The workmen were quite respectful. I'm a grown woman and I won't be a prisoner."

"All right, all right," María said, and gazed silently

out the window at the grey sky pressing down on the grey city, seeming to enclose its inhabitants in an invisible but inescapable prison.

* * *

"It's so hot," María said, fanning herself in the front seat of Dr. Mendoza's big black Chevrolet and lifting her dark brown hair up off her neck. It was January—high summer in Lima—the temperature approaching 80 degrees. The sun shone briefly on the unwatered coastal sands of this part of the campus. Green and flowering oases, small islands of color in a sea of barren dirt, surrounded some of the buildings. Next to the functional steel of the Language Center, hibiscus, roses, marigolds bordered a swath of green grass. And in the middle of campus, a big stand of corn grew in the groundskeeper's garden next to his small adobe house where chickens, dog, and children played in the dirt. But vast stretches of campus were barren sand.

We drove across campus to a more modernly equipped building where I was to show my class a National Geographic tape on the Nazca Lines.

María was riveted, not by the program, but by the ads.

"Look, look!" María said, as a glamorous woman descended a curving staircase and swirled through an elegant home, intoxicated by the advertised perfume.

María sat erect on the edge of her seat absorbing images of leafy streets and well groomed dogs, adorable children in splendid homes demanding certain brands of cereal, trim and perfectly coiffed housewives ecstatic because clothes they pulled from gleaming machines were pristine white. Like children, both she and Dr. Mendoza exclaimed out loud at each thrilling image.

Afterwards, as Dr. Mendoza drove us to our bus stops under the grey Lima sky, María looked out at the turbulent, garbage strewn avenue. Black exhaust from buses rumbling by fouled the air. A beggar dressed in tattered filthy rags, wearing a TV antenna on his head, crossed the dirty street, talking to himself. A gust of wind sent scraps of paper skittering through the dust.

"There is nothing here for me," she said, leaning back against the worn seat of the big old Chevy and looking straight ahead. "My friend lives in Miami. I'll save money to go to her. Then when the little ones are bigger, I'll leave this place."

Her youngest children, Niki and Lourdes, the one "with problems," were twelve and fourteen.

* * *

Niki, the baby, was just a child when I first arrived in Peru. My last trip back, she had become a young woman of 23, yet so much younger than her sisters at that age.

"I fled when I saw him with his face all twisted, eyes staring," María had said that last visit. "I couldn't bear it, so I never went back.

"I have a friend now. He lives in the neighborhood. Just a friend, but he built this for me," María said, showing me her new kitchen. It was no longer the dark, windowless room at the near end of the house as it had been when I first met María. Now adjacent to the living room, her kitchen faced the tiny courtyard. Though still small, with a heavy worn stove and chipped enamel sink, it was bright and open.

Niki had just come home from work, wearing the

pants set I had brought her from the States, even though it was too warm for the heavy sweater, and a few beads of sweat pearled on her forehead. Teresa, too, had arrived for lunch. Lourdes smiled vacantly at the group. María chatted while she lifted heavy iron lids and inspected or stirred the contents of the big heavy pots.

"He is alone and I cook for him, but that's all. He has his seat at the dinner table. Niki was so jealous of him. She tried to push him out of his chair."

We all laughed, but Niki was unmoved. Tall and slim, beautiful at 23, she was still the baby, frisking like a foal in the kitchen.

* * *

From time to time now María calls. She called the other day. Lourdes, the next to the youngest daughter, in her late twenties, the one with problems, had died. The doctors had made a mistake.

"Niki doesn't know. She thinks her sister is still in the hospital."

Niki, the vivacious, playful one, has a benign tumor on her spine, but María doesn't dare let the doctors operate, for the procedure is very dangerous. She doesn't have the money, of course, to bring Niki to the United States.

"She is blind and cannot move," María said, "and I have to turn her every few hours, around the clock, to prevent bed sores."

Just the two of them are left now in the small house.

Still holding the phone in one hand, the dial tone insistent, I see María in her little house not far from the sea. The bell rings and she runs to the garage, for she has turned it into a *tienda* with its iron grate protecting the little store of sodas, crackers, candy, a few canned goods. She sells the two workmen Cokes and waits anxiously behind the iron grill for them to return the bottles.

"Gracias, Señora," says the one returning the bottles.

María looks out through the bars at the small adobe houses across the dusty unpaved street. The store dominates one corner of the garage; in another stands a pay phone neighbors can use for a small fee. A nearby resident rents the remaining half of the garage to lock his car into at night. Just a few streets over is the sea, restlessly rolling against the Port of Callao, grey sea merging into a vast grey sky horizonless. But from here María cannot see it.

She goes back inside and gently lifts Niki, the tallest of her daughters, and turns her over. Niki's long legs, thin as a newborn colt's, sprawl across the mattress.

"Mamá," she says, smiling blindly up at María.

El Jefe del Departamento de Inglés

A short broad man with a genial, dignified air scanned the group straggling into the small airport, blinking in the bright lights. Small children clung to their parents, Peruvians coming to visit relatives or returning home. Four athletic young men in shorts, vests, and hiking boots strode jauntily forward, no doubt here to hike the Inca Trail, as more and more foreigners were now doing. A slim woman professionally dressed in a brown business suit and high heels struggled under the weight of an overstuffed backpack. Her long strawberry blonde hair was braided and piled high on her head like a crown. Her tall son, perhaps fifteen, presented a sharp contrast. In a black suit and red tie, with dark brown, nearly black, hair and eyes, he looked almost Peruvian. He, too, wore a backpack, and in his arms carried an army duffle bag folded in half and tied with rope. The woman looked around uncertainly.

"Ms. Wulferson?" The broad man stepped forward. He was wearing charcoal slacks and sweater and a white shirt with a wide gray-striped tie. "I'm Dr. Mendoza. How was your flight? Not too tiring, I hope."

His English was excellent, with a pronounced Texas accent, for he had studied at the University of Texas in his youth and spoke familiarly of Austin.

"This way," he said, ushering them to baggage claims. Her son dragged four large trunks off the conveyor belt, all four badly dented and two smashed askew. The woman rolled her eyes, and all three burst out laughing.

Customs began by going through each of the trunks, but by the fourth waved it on with some asperity. The woman looked embarrassed.

"We tried to pack for a year . . . ," she began, but Dr. Mendoza urged her on without replying.

Outside the entrance to the terminal, a crowd surged forward, many angrily waving signs. The tension was palpable, fear drenching the air. Dr. Mendoza silently hustled the woman and her son forward through the crowd, looking neither to the right nor left, but straight ahead.

The streets of Lima were dark under a light drizzle as the big black sixties Chevrolet sped through the night. Señora Mendoza sat silent in the front seat, while in the back seat Dr. Mendoza's assistant, María, held Margaret Wulferson's hand and patted her son's arm, claiming these visitors from another world.

It was now past midnight, and the lines of Dr. Mendoza's face grew taut as he drove up and down streets in a dark and silent neighborhood, searching for the home where the university had reserved a room for the woman and her son.

At last he found it. The boy easily lifted the heavy trunks from the back of the Chevy, and he and the woman carried them up the winding staircase.

"I have a bad back," Dr. Mendoza had begun, but the woman smoothly grabbed one end of a trunk, her son holding the bottom end as they trotted up the stairs.

A few polite words to the landlady, a farewell to Margaret Wulferson, and Dr. Mendoza sped off into the dark, racing to make it home before the 1:00 A.M. curfew. María would have to spend the night with them. The soldiers in the streets would hold strictly to the rules, professor or no professor. Young kids, many of them, carelessly holding rifles for the first time. Just the day before, a bomb had gone off in the central city, showering diners in an expensive restaurant with glass, injuring several, but thanks be to God, killing no one. Dr. Mendoza grew solemn as he contemplated the rising power of Sendero Luminoso, the Shining Path, a Maoist group, and Tupac Amaru, a rebel group named after the last hold-out Inca ruler.

Two days later Dr. Mendoza pulled up before the house in Miraflores where he had left Margaret Wulferson and her son. The university often housed visiting professors here, but usually for just a few days or weeks. This young woman, however, had been hired to teach in the English department for a year.

Dr. Mendoza spoke into the intercom, and after he heard the lock release, he and María walked through the door in the high stone wall topped by jagged broken glass.

The maid unlocked the triple-locked house door, and they entered the foyer.

Señora Yolanda was all smiles as she welcomed Dr. Mendoza and María, then hurriedly sent the maid to call Ms. Wulferson. She came down the stairs, her son at her side. He was a tall handsome boy, today dressed in jeans and a red short-sleeved knit shirt.

"You'll be cold," Señora Yolanda said to the boy. July, mid-winter in Peru, and the temperature was in the sixties.

"He'll be okay," his mother said. The boy didn't speak Spanish, and his mother barely enough to get by.

Dr. Mendoza took the broad Paseo de la Republica to downtown, then exited through the crowded streets of El Centro, old Lima. Beggars and street vendors, campesinos from the Andes, swarmed the streets of the central city, blocking the sidewalks and spilling into the streets. Ancient Fords and Chevrolets competed with big buses belching black smoke and with occasional sleek new Toyotas.

At an intersection, an old woman in long graying braids and the full dark skirt of the campesina, thrust a pack of chewing gum through the window, beseeching Dr. Mendoza to buy some.

"No, thank you," he replied in English.

The old woman looked startled and a little baffled. Switching languages, she said, "Are you American?"

The light changed and as he drove through the intersection, Dr. Mendoza laughed out loud.

"Even the street vendors speak English."

Across the Rimac River from El Centro, on the northern edge of the city, the university abutted steep barren hills rising abruptly from the flat dry coastal sands. Simple adobe houses, in various stages of construction, were etched into the sheer sides of the hills, houses of poor campesinos drawn to the capital city from high in the Andes. In front of the university ran a major thoroughfare. From it, Dr. Mendoza turned right and drove through a gate in the far end of the wall that surrounded the university.

Ms. Wulferson and her son followed Dr. Mendoza and María, clanging up the steel staircase and along the steel walkway of the second floor of a grimy functional building till they reached the Language Center. Here in one large open space Dr. Mendoza had his office/classroom and María the language lab, her domain. Separate from the main function of the university—to produce engineers—the English department had still a necessary role, for engineering texts the world over are written in English, the British and Americans dominating the field.

Ms. Wulferson's class waited in a nearby classroom. Standing before the assembled group, slightly rocked back on his heels, Dr. Mendoza introduced Ms. Wulferson, warmly welcomed her to the university and said at great length how fortunate they all were to have her here. He also introduced the boy as her son, then with a flourish turned the floor over to her.

Ms. Wulferson said she was happy to be there and looked forward to the class. The young men and one woman sat attentive and expectant, waiting, but she said nothing more and looked flustered.

Very smoothly, Dr. Mendoza joined her in front of the class and said that now it was time to take a tour of the university.

Unlike the strictly utilitarian classroom buildings, the main building that housed the rector—the president of the university—was a handsome rust and cream colored building. Guards unlocked heavy wooden doors and escorted Dr. Mendoza and his retinue down a long hall lined with paintings to a large ornate door flanked by metal sculptures. More guards unlocked the carved wooden doors and admitted the group into the inner chambers. Although several secretaries were present, a hush pervaded these rooms.

"Oh, there you are," Dr. Mendoza said in English, as they suddenly encountered the rector in the inner hallway.

The rector was a graceful, slender man, superficially polite but remote and forbidding. Pausing briefly in the hallway, he spoke all the ceremonial Spanish phrases welcoming Ms. Wulferson to the university, but coldly, hardly glancing at her.

"Why don't you use your English?" Dr. Mendoza suggested, but the rector continued in Spanish. He had been ill with a cold and had just returned to work. He still sounded a little stuffy. Both Dr. Mendoza and Dr. Olivarez, the vice-rector, a large plump man full of smiles who had joined them to meet with the rector, expressed sorrow at the rector's illness. As the rector continued his formal speech, Dr. Mendoza translated. In English, the words sounded flowery, but every line of the rector's body and lineament of his face sent a message of intimidation and dismissal. He did not invite the group into his office, merely paused in the hallway to make the ceremonial welcome. When he had concluded the brief ceremony, he simply turned his back on them and walked off, leaving Ms. Wulferson speechless.

"He is Spanish," the plump vice-rector whispered reverently into the ear of Ms. Wulferson as the rector disappeared down the hallway.

"Come," Dr. Mendoza said heartily, "it's time for lunch."

The next day Dr. Mendoza, his wife Angeles, and María, in the big black Chevrolet, arrived at the house in Miraflores.

"This is the route," Dr. Mendoza said, skillfully following a big belching bus from its stop a few blocks from the Miraflores house all the way to the Plaza 2 de Mayo, a major downtown intersection. Margaret and her son sat silent in the back seat.

"Here is where I will pick you up."

Eight streets, like the spokes of a wheel, entered the circle of the Plaza 2 de Mayo, with cars honking and weaving across traffic at high speed. Pedestrians thronged the sidewalks and forced their way through the gauntlet of vendors' carts and deft pickpockets. Flies clotted putrid pools of rot. The streets were awash in garbage, swarming with people, and in the air throbbed the energy and excitement arising from masses of people desperately trying to survive, where anything might happen.

He worried about her, a young woman, a mother. Americans didn't know Peru. For the first week, he would pick her up at the Miraflores house. Eventually she would learn how to take the bus all the way to this plaza by herself, where he could pick her up for the final leg of the journey. But still he worried.

Having shown Ms. Wulferson the way by following an actual bus, Dr. Mendoza retraced the route back to the wealthy Miraflores suburb. But now he stopped at a restaurant across from Kennedy Park, not far from the grey sea lapping at the shores of Lima under a grey sky.

"Four coffees," Dr. Mendoza said to the waiter, "and . . ." He paused and looked at the boy.

"Orange juice, please."

Dr. Mendoza had chosen a table far from the windows, and from time to time glanced quickly toward the door, at the windows, then protectively at the group around him.

Outside, the evening air was fresh and cool as the group strolled through the park afterwards, looking at paintings on display along the sidewalks: scenes of the Amazon with Indians paddling dugout canoes; of the altiplano with its herds of startled vicunas; of a campesina leading a llama, red ribbons in its hair, down the stone streets of Cuzco high in the Andes.

"Dr. Mendoza," a man approaching the group said in English. He almost bowed. "How are you? It's so good to see you."

"How have you been? My former student," Dr. Mendoza added to the others.

"Wonderful. I'm an American citizen now, about to retire from the military. In fact I served in Vietnam. You changed my life. None of this would have been possible without Dr. Mendoza," he said, turning to his wife and young daughter.

Dr. Mendoza beamed. "No one deserves it more."

A car sped down the adjacent street, tires slightly squealing as it made the turn toward a metallic sea fretting the city shore under a colorless sky. Both men stepped closer to their women, eyes scanning the crowd, then after a moment relaxed.

"It's late," Dr. Mendoza said, exchanging final pleasantries and ushering his little group toward the old Chevy.

One morning when Ms. Wulferson was late in coming down, Señora Yolanda sat with Dr. Mendoza while he waited.

"That was terrible last night," she said, "the bombing."

"The one at the restaurant across from Kennedy Park? We were there just a few days ago."

Señora Yolanda looked solemn. "I heard there was blood everywhere from the shattered glass, but no one killed."

"Several were carried to the hospital," Dr. Mendoza said. "Early this morning a car bomb destroyed a limousine in front of the American Embassy."

"Tomorrow will be worse, I'm afraid."

"Yes, the anniversary of Sendero Luminoso will be. . . Oh, good morning," Dr. Mendoza said as Ms. Wulferson and her son descended the staircase. He looked significantly at Señora Yolanda.

"Buenos días, Señora," said Señora Yolanda.

Ms. Wulferson looked from one to the other, but neither Dr. Mendoza nor Señora Yolanda would say anything more.

Ms. Wulferson had been teaching just a week when Dr. Mendoza interrupted her class with an apology but said everyone had to leave immediately.

"The rector has cancelled all classes and locked the gates to the university. The guards will let us out, but we must go quickly."

The students gathered up their papers and vanished. Ms. Wulferson hastened after Dr. Mendoza and María. He paused until she caught up. She was his responsibility. Her son strode alongside, taller than the others, looking curiously about. For now he accompanied her to classes, which everyone thought very natural for a fifteen-year-old boy.

Activist students thronged the sidewalks just outside the university gates, many holding signs aloft. On the thoroughfare itself, other students were dripping oil and setting fire to old tires. Dr. Mendoza exited a gate at the far end, away from the tires. No one said anything.

"Our appointment with the cultural attaché is for later this afternoon, so we will get there a little early—on American time, not Latin time," Dr. Mendoza said with a droll smile as he skillfully drove the big black Chevrolet down the narrow streets of El Centro.

The United States Information Service was housed in a small colonial building in the old city. In the thick plate glass of the heavy outer door, shatter lines radiated out from a bullet hole in its center. A guard opened the door and ushered Ms. Wulferson and her son, Dr. Mendoza and María, into a handsome conference room with a massive table almost the length of the large room. The American Embassy, of which the Information Service was a part, had agreed to pay half of Ms. Wulferson's university salary. Dr. Mendoza was also hoping to get some materials for his English lab.

Caroline, the cultural attaché, a slim attractive woman, entered the room and shook hands all around.

"Welcome to Lima," she said, her warm smile embracing the boy as well as Margaret Wulferson. "You may experience a delayed culture shock here. In many ways the city looks modern, with freeways and banks and upscale grocery stores, especially in wealthy suburbs like Miraflores. But the culture is different, and people's reactions may seem stranger and more frustrating the longer you stay."

Caroline's eyes sparkled and she smiled frequently at the handsome fifteen-year-old sitting quietly at the table, absorbing everything.

"Peruvians spend the largest part of their money on food, but their second highest expenditure is on education. You will find many students from the poorer classes at the university. I'll put you in touch with the Director of the Binational Center and with the Director of the Fulbright Commission. I'm sure you can get materials for the Language Center from them," she said directly to Margaret Wulferson.

Dr. Mendoza sat quietly, withdrawing into himself, saying nothing. Here Ms. Wulferson seemed to him another person, a larger than life representative of the awesome power of the United States.

"If you should need anything at all, just ask," Caroline said, hugging both Margaret and the boy. She smiled warmly at the two of them, then finally turned to shake hands with Dr. Mendoza and María.

"Thank you," Dr. Mendoza said deferentially to Caroline. The slim young woman half his age nodded.

The four exited the handsome and well appointed USIS office into another world. The gray overcast seemed to enclose them in a pall of diesel exhaust and gas fumes. The boy began to cough as they walked down the grimy sidewalk to Dr. Mendoza's big black Chevy.

"Don't forget your appointment with Dr. Lopez tomorrow," María said.

"See how she bosses me around," Dr. Mendoza said to Ms. Wulferson.

"No, no, I mother him," María said, walking briskly down the sidewalk. "That's my job."

Dr. Lopez was director of the university's mathematical institute and close associate of the rector. Asked to hire Margaret Wulferson by a member of one of Peru's powerful families, who like him traced their ancestry directly to Spain, the rector had deputed the responsibility to Dr. Lopez, who frequently housed visiting mathematics professors at the home in Miraflores. He had made the arrangements, but had turned over responsibility for Ms. Wulferson to Dr. Mendoza. Dr. Lopez had understood from the rector's tone that the American was an obligation, but not a pleasant one. The meeting was in fulfillment of the obligation.

The next day before the afternoon meeting, Dr. Lopez, a slender graceful man, made one of his rare appearances in the faculty dining hall. He sat at a table with three other distinguished-looking men. Dr. Mendoza led Ms. Wulferson and María up to the table. He stood quietly near Dr. Lopez, at the edge of the table, looking down at the floor, hands clasped together. Dr. Lopez continued an animated conversation for some time before finally turning toward Dr. Mendoza in simulated surprise, as though just now aware of his presence.

"Let me present Ms. Wulferson," Dr. Mendoza said, gracefully, but still with humility.

"Enchanted. I hope you are enjoying your stay at the university."

The other men at the table took no notice of the proceedings.

"We will see you in my office at 2:00," Dr. Lopez continued, speaking directly to Dr. Mendoza.

That afternoon, Ingrid, Dr. Lopez's strikingly beautiful and highly ornamental secretary, ushered them into the office. Dr. Lopez had just spoken a few words of welcome when the building suddenly began to shake violently, so violently it seemed the rattling glass windows must shatter.

"My children!" María screamed, and ran to Margaret Wulferson, who sat quietly. Margaret put her arm around María and held her until she quit shaking. As abruptly as it had started, the quaking ceased.

"That's just how women are," Dr. Mendoza said grandly,"so afraid of earthquakes." He smiled patronizingly at the women.

Ms.Wulferson's face colored and her nostrils flared.

"My wife runs wildly through the house during earthquakes, but my daughter doesn't pay any attention at all to them," Dr. Lopez said mildly.

Ms. Wulferson's face relaxed and she smiled at María.

"I will need to have my visa renewed in a couple of months," she said to Dr. Lopez.

"You must go to the American Embassy for them to take care of it."

("The American Embassy can do nothing," Caroline said when Margaret went to her, "as Dr. Lopez knows very well.")

Dr. Mendoza stood, followed by the women, and thanked Dr. Lopez for his time.

"It was a pleasure," Dr. Lopez said, gracefully ushering them from his office to the anteroom, where Ingrid, who seemed to have no other duties, waited to escort them to the outer hallway.

From the main building the three drove to the bursar's office to see if Margaret's first check was ready.

"This is Ms. Wulferson," Dr. Mendoza said formally, with dignified mien, his broad body erect.

They waited outside the cashier's cage while the clerk thumbed through a pile of papers.

"Your passport, please. You must sign these papers here, here, and here. And that one on this line, please, and the other one here and there and the third . . ."

"How have you been," María was saying to one clerk while the other witnessed the signing of the papers and Dr. Mendoza translated. Then the chief clerk formally presented the check to Ms. Wulferson. Dr. Mendoza and María thanked the clerks, María effusively, Dr. Mendoza with genial formality. Ms. Wulferson added her thanks.

Dr. Mendoza walked solemnly down the steps to the black Chevy, María on one side, Ms. Wulferson on the other. Once inside the car, Dr. Mendoza and María began bouncing up and down in their seats.

"Wonderful!"

"I can't believe it!"

From the back seat, Margaret stared at them.

"You just don't know," María said, intercepting her look.

(In the months to come, Margaret Wulferson would find out. Strikes shut down the university and no checks were cut for months. University records—student transcripts—she learned, were three years behind.)

"Let's have a coffee," Dr. Mendoza said, feeling celebratory one afternoon. "I have an errand to run for my wife downtown."

As the three walked down the sidewalk, a door opened in the wall surrounding the university and a small woman with weathered skin and wrinkled face rolled a heavy vendor's cart out onto the sidewalk. Dr. Mendoza reached out to help her and his face softened. There flashed into his mind the memory of his mother, pushing just such a cart onto the street every morning.

Little Lui Mendoza bringing home his school report, his eyes shining. "My prince," his mother said, enfolding him in her arms, her wrinkled and weathered face softening. Light from the open door barely illuminated the dark kitchen. She had been cooking when he ran in from the street, and the smells made his stomach rumble. She smiled as she filled a bowl with rice and ladled the hot stew on top. From the back room came the drunken snores of his father. He looked quickly up at his mother. "Don't worry. He won't wake up for a long time," his mother said.

"Can we stop at the store?" María asked as they walked to the big black Chevy.

"What? Oh, yes, of course."

Rotting garbage lay in the median of the thoroughfare running past the university wall; an intermittent breeze fluttered pieces of paper littering the barren sand. Heavy buses rumbled past, spewing thick black clouds of diesel exhaust.

A man lay propped against the curb, his legs extending out into the street where the big buses thundered past. His unkempt hair and long beard were grizzled, and he was covered with dust, his clothes merely shredded rags. The position of the man seemed to say, "Let a bus run over my legs; nothing can be worse than it already is." Or perhaps, "Let it crush my legs. At least then someone will have to take care of me."

"Who does he think he is, Moses?" Dr. Mendoza said in English. Then, "He was in love, but he was disappointed."

Margaret Wulferson cringed as they passed the man. She looked down at his legs, covered in dusty rags, so vulnerable stretched out on the dirty asphalt, with monstrous buses rumbling by.

The three walked several blocks past the university along the thoroughfare until they reached a spot where freelance mechanics had set up on its unusually broad median under the colorless grey sky. One man had dug a pit in the sand; others had racks of car parts scattered in the dust. A light breeze fluttered loose scraps of paper across the dingy sand of the median. Early that morning Dr. Mendoza had left his big black Chevy with one of the mechanics, and now it was ready to go.

"I also need to get my iron repaired," María said. "Will we have time?"

"Certainly," Dr. Mendoza said. He and Señora Mendoza, childless themselves, were godparents to one of María's eight daughters, Teresa. María and her children, like Dr. Mendoza's relatives and his wife's relatives and now Margaret Wulferson, were his responsibilities.

As they were returning to the car, errands completed, they came upon one of the street people cadging tips by washing windshields. He was putting on quite a show. Heading his dirty rag like a comic Pelé onto the windshield of a car stopped at the intersection, whooshing it around with jerky movements like a speeded-up movie reel, he had the whole street as his audience, and the two young women inside the car were cracking up with laughter. Margaret Wulferson paused to watch, and she and María were smiling, but Dr. Mendoza turned away, as though averting his gaze from a disreputable sight, and strode faster down the sidewalk.

Dr. Mendoza's big black sixties Chevrolet was a sturdy, reliable car, a measure of his status, but once again it needed repair, and this time the mechanic kept it for several days. During this time, the three caught a bus together from the university to the downtown, often transferring on Avenida Garciloso de la Vega to their respective buses, Margaret to Miraflores, María to La Perla near the Port of Callao, and Dr. Mendoza to Magdalena, his house also close to the cold grey Pacific.

Most days after work Dr. Mendoza had treated María and Ms. Wulferson to coffee, sometimes pie as well, and for the last two days had bought their bus tickets when they boarded at the university. This day Margaret gaily bought the three tickets as she boarded first. They cost the equivalent of perhaps a quarter apiece, but she thought it would be a small gesture of appreciation.

Dr. Mendoza's face darkened when she smiled and held out the tickets, and he had nothing to say for the rest of the trip, averting his gaze from her.

"Poor María," Dr. Mendoza said to Ms. Wulferson one morning as they sat on either side of his metal desk at the back of his classroom. "She won't be in today. One of her daughters is ill. It's so hard for her. My wife and I do what we can."

"What happened to her husband?"

"He left her for another woman. Deserted his family. Now he's living in Venezuela and has more children. What can she do?"

His broad face expressed solemn resignation. His ears were a distinctive shape, large with pendulous earlobes. "Inca ears," Ms. Wulferson's son had remarked to her. His short squat body must have been powerful in his youth, so different in conformation from the slim elegant bodies of the rector and Dr. Lopez, yet he carried himself with a dignified authority.

"All she can do is work and care for her daughters. Tomorrow, however, I am inviting you and your son and María to come to my house for the evening."

In the suburb of Magdalena del Mar, a damp breeze from the cold Pacific brushed the shoulders of María and Ms. Wulferson and her son as they stood before the door of Dr. Mendoza's house.

"Come in, come in," Dr. Mendoza boomed from behind his sister, who had opened the door. She was a small, wizened, retiring woman, very different from her large extroverted brother.

Geraniums and variegated tropical plants grew inside a small interior courtyard, one of whose walls was entirely of glass. Gorgeous Moorish tiles formed the bottom half of the other three glass walls. An exposed stairway led to the second floor of the large house, with a breakfast nook underneath it facing the little interior garden.

"This way, this way," Dr. Mendoza said heartily, leading his guests into the living room. Señora Mendoza sat on a couch before a large stone fireplace, unusual for Lima, where most homes have no heating or cooling.

"We got the idea for it from our time in the States," Dr. Mendoza said, gesturing grandly toward the fireplace. "It's nice when a cold wind blows across the Pacific and a damp fog settles in."

A large color TV and stereo dominated one corner of the room. On the walls hung still lifes, Señora Mendoza's paintings.

"Here are more of Angeles' paintings," Dr. Mendoza said, noticing Ms. Wulferson gazing at the ones in the living room and leading her back out into the entrance hall and the breakfast nook. Señora Angeles and María followed.

"And here is the laundry room." Dr. Mendoza gazed with pride at the modern washer and dryer, rare in Peru. "I have had to fight for everything I have," he said, almost to himself.

Outside, an uncompleted three-storey apartment building rose from the dust of their large lot. They walked through the shell of the building, picking their way carefully through empty echoing rooms.

"The zoning rules kept changing," Dr. Mendoza said, staring at the blank walls of the empty rooms. "The bureaucracy is terrible."

"At first they said it was all right," Señora Mendoza added, "but then different inspectors stopped the construction. We were never able to get past the red tape."

"And here," Dr. Mendoza said, pointing directly behind the house, is where I wanted to build a language school."

For a moment he stood silent, dreaming the old dream. A damp breeze from the cold Pacific stirred the air, and the fine dust of the coastal sands beneath their feet covered their shoes. The perpetually grey sky darkened and the colorless light dimmed.

In the kitchen, plates of sandwiches and cake sat on a comfortably worn wooden table. Dr. Mendoza's wizened sister was stirring hot chocolate on the stove, and a pot of coffee stood steaming nearby.

The sister did not sit at the table with the rest of them but perched on a stool by the counter, stirring sugar into her coffee, and did not speak.

"When we were in the States, a big design firm wanted to hire Angeles, but she didn't want to stay in America."

"They offered to hire Luis as an accountant. We would have made a lot of money, but I couldn't live away from my family. Some things are more important than wealth."

"Now Angeles has her own sewing school downtown where she teaches the elements of design."

The boy had wandered off to the living room. He was reading an old Reader's Digest when it was time to go. The sister was sweeping leaves off the walk, content in her own world also.

"I came so close," Dr. Mendoza said. "I missed the passing score by just a few points." He was driving María and Ms Wulferson along Abancay Avenue in El Centro—old Lima—with its once grand plazas, its graceful balconies overhanging narrow streets, but its air now fouled and its ancient buildings begrimed.

His ambition had been to be a UN translator, but though he spoke English extremely well, with a regional

American accent, no trace of a Spanish one, and maneuvered well in either language, he could not translate well enough between the two cultures.

"We will miss you so much, Lui," his mother had said, so many long years ago, "but you are our hope. You are my treasure." His mother and sister had cried, and so had he.

Sunny Austin in the early fifties, so clean and open, with its magnificent university and impressive capitol, the two buildings defining the skyline and the city. It was his chance and he had seized it, studying hard and doing quite well.

"Let me help you with that, Mrs. Jackson," he said, unloading the box from the back of the station wagon and carrying it into the living room. He read the instructions and set up the TV while she watched from the couch.

"I declare, you are such a helpful young man, Luis," said his landlady. "I don't know what I would do without you."

She insisted that he watch a program with her. Austin had just gotten its first television station, and soon he was laughing uproariously at episodes of *I Love Lucy*.

"You're a hard worker, Luis," his landlady said once, "not like some of these students. You don't drink, do you?"

"No, ma'm," he said, and his young face grew stern.

"Here we are," Dr. Mendoza said, suddenly seeing the grimy downtown building that housed the radio station. He let María and Ms. Wulferson out while he drove around to the entrance to the parking garage.

He had thought he could record a tape Ms. Wulferson had brought on his home equipment and make it compatible with the university recorder. She had given him the tape a month ago. There was plenty of time. However, she kept mentioning it. So the night before she was to use it in class, he made the new tape. But for some reason it didn't work. He tried again a few days later. This time the volume was so low the tape was almost inaudible. So he had decided to visit Radio Union with its more advanced equipment, a station where he had once worked. He hosted a Sunday program on Argentinean tangos at another station now, but was still good friends with Radio Union's manager.

The two women were watching as he came down the ramp empty-handed.

"I was sure I had it with me. I don't know what happened to it."

"I didn't see it when you came in this morning," María said.

"I must have left it at home."

Before them, as they stepped out of the ancient creaking elevator onto the dingy fourth floor of the radio building, a crowd of people surged against a partially opened door. A heavy bar locked the door in place, leaving an aperture of barely eight inches through which people handed money and the messages they wanted aired to an armed guard inside.

"Do you know why security is so tight?" Dr. Mendoza asked. "They're terrified terrorists will force their way in and with a pistol to the head make them broadcast a message."

He handed through his journalist's ID and asked for the manager.

"I'm sorry, but he's not in."

"Please show him my identification."

Reluctantly the secretary departed, intimidated by the tone of authority. The guard held back the heaving throng as the secretary briefly unbolted the heavy door.

"Dr. Mendoza," the manager said, embracing him.

"Allow me to present Professor Wulferson and Señora María. Señor García, the station chief."

"Mucho gusto."

"Encantada."

"I would like to come by tomorrow to make a copy of a tape for Professor Wulferson to use in her class."

"Wonderful," the manager said, delighted to see Dr. Mendoza, and no one, with the exception of Ms. Wulferson, found it strange that Dr. Mendoza had come by in order to say he was coming by the next day.

A flurry of wind lifted fragments of paper from a pile of garbage lingering in the sandy median of the large thoroughfare in front of the university. Driving María and Ms. Wulferson toward downtown, Dr. Mendoza saw a small boy of ten fall in the middle of the street. A car squealed and skidded to a stop just before running over him. The boy rolled to his feet and scampered the rest of the way across, then darted back to retrieve the large bundle he had dropped.

"Is he hurt?" María cried.

"What happened?" called Margaret Wulferson from the back seat.

Dr. Mendoza had stopped in the middle of the street. He jumped out and rushed to the little boy. The child's leg was badly scraped, he had banged his head, and he seemed shaken up, but he had set off down the sidewalk.

"Son," Dr. Mendoza called out, "Are you hurt?"

The boy turned back.

"No, I just fell running across." He shuddered, remembering the car looming over him as he lay helpless on the pavement. "I'm on my way home," he said, thinking quickly, "but I don't have money for bus fare."

Dr. Mendoza reached into his pocket and handed the boy all the change he had. "Be careful, son."

"Muchas gracias, Señor," the boy said, his face lighting up.

A rough looking man crossed from the far side of the street and confronted Dr. Mendoza just as he returned to his car.

"So you hit the boy with your big car and pay him to be quiet," he said nastily. "Think you can get away with that?"

María leapt out of the car. "Unjust! He tries to help the child. Such injustice!" She was shouting now.

Dr. Mendoza tried to get her back in the car, but she was too angry.

"I am a witness," the man said to Dr. Mendoza, ignoring María.

"How can you say such things!" she yelled.

"Let's go to the police station, then," Dr. Mendoza said.

"I saw it happen."

"Fine. Let's go to the police station."

María looked from one to the other.

"Let's go to the police station. You can tell your story there," Dr. Mendoza repeated quietly, looking straight at the rough looking man. "Let's go."

The man grew pale, turned on his heel, and slunk away.

Dr. Mendoza had not been feeling well lately. Frequently he had to stop to find a bathroom, and urination was painful. That night as he walked to the dinner table, he suddenly doubled over in pain, unable to move.

"Luis!" Angeles ran to him, and she and his sister struggled to get him on the couch. Angeles called the ambulance.

The medicine had eased the pain, and as he lay on the worn sheets of the hospital bed, he expected to see death leering at him from a corner of the room.

His father's body, laid out in the small dark living room, the only light filtering through a dusty windowpane. A few neighbors gathered around, his mother's closest friend holding her hand. How could his mother cry? His father's face was yellowed and the cheeks hollowed. The fingernails black and broken. The body grimed with the soot and dust of the street. Luis turned away in horror and disgust.

He slept.

"Prostate trouble," the doctor said. "You'll be okay, but you should have come in sooner."

He prayed and gave thanks to God, then slept some more.

In the afternoon, María and Ms. Wulferson came.

"Oh, thank you for coming," he said, choking up. They waited while he wiped away the tears. "I am so glad to be alive."

The next day the doctors released him, and the day after, María and Ms. Wulferson visited him at home. Dr. Mendoza was sitting in an easy chair in the living room in front of the warm fireplace, a beige and brown blanket draped over his knees.

"How are you?" María asked.

"Much better."

"I'm glad to see you looking well," Ms. Wulferson said.

This was the moment, he thought.

"Thank you." He took a deep breath. "May I call you Margaret?"

"Of course."

Dr. Mendoza flushed with pleasure. He waited expectantly, but she didn't say anything more. He had expected her to say, "And shall I call you Luis?" or "What would you like for me to call you?" He was Luis or Lucho to his family and close friends or even sometimes Lui to his sister. This defining moment, when first names replaced the formal address of colleagues, signaling the intimacy of friendship, did not seem so dramatic to Margaret. He couldn't help feeling a little disappointed.

Luis leaned back in his chair. He had finished correcting a set of papers and had stacked them neatly on one side of the desk. English exercises on the dusty chalk board at the other end of the room were slightly smudged where someone's coat sleeve had rubbed against them. All was quiet in María's half of the room where the rows of language cubicles with their large-reel tapes stood, for she had not come in to work today. Her next-to-the-last child, Lourdes, the one with problems, was sick again. So sad. Luis was waiting for Margaret to finish her class. He hated to be alone.

"Oh, there you are. How about a coffee?"

He could see her hesitate.

"Thank you," she said finally.

A blooming hibiscus and two red roses were bright against the green of the small irrigated patch of ground surrounding the Language Department Building. They walked across a swath of barren sand, dust settling on their shoes, to the small restaurant, its adobe walls shedding dark green paint. All four tables were vacant. The ageless proprietor, her worn skin a grayish brown, greeted Dr. Mendoza warmly, then left with their order.

"Poor María. Caring for all those daughters all alone. And Lourdes sick again. But what can she do? Her husband deserted her," Luis said with an air of tragedy. He took a sip of his coffee.

"But she's done such a good job," Margaret said.

"Yes, but so much work, here and at home. Such a struggle, no man to help her." A look of sudden suspicion crossed his face. "Not that we know . . . "

Margaret didn't speak, but the look on her face said it all. Luis reconsidered. Women could be deceitful, he knew, but really, surely María was true.

"So sad. Such a burden, eight daughters. But her husband left her. What can she do? A life of sorrow. So sad, yet inescapable."

Margaret focused on her coffee, the smooth mild Peruvian coffee, and did not speak.

Outside, the high gray overcast held them captive in its dome as they walked to the big black Chevy. The cold Humboldt Current, paralleling Lima's shores, swept past the crowded throbbing city, dampening the air.

"Please let me out here," Margaret said, as they reached downtown on Garciloso de la Vega.

He had planned to take her closer to the Miraflores suburb, where a single bus ride would get her comfortably home.

"Oh, why?"

"I have an errand to run."

"But what is it?"

"This next corner will do fine," she said firmly.

"I would be glad to take you any place . . . ," he began, but she was already opening the car door.

"Thank you," she said, and hurried across the street.

Errand accomplished, Margaret caught the next bus to Miraflores. In this city of seven million, one could travel from one place to any other destination in the city without walking more than a few blocks. Buses were often extremely crowded, but this day Margaret found a seat beside a pleasant-faced middle-aged woman, who soon engaged her in conversation.

"Do you have a husband and children?

"A son, but no husband. I'm divorced," Margaret said.

"Ah, yes. My husband left me with five small children—a long time ago.

"Who remembers?" she added cheerily.

Seated around the comfortably worn kitchen table, Luis smiled expansively at the women—Angeles, María, Margaret. His sister unobtrusively refilled the coffee cups, then returned to her stool next to the counter. Margaret's son was watching TV in the living room.

A month and a half ago Luis had come up with an ambitious plan for Margaret to teach an intensive eight-week course to be offered to junior faculty from other universities.

"Just think," he had said to Margaret, "you can have students from all over Peru in your class."

He had made an appointment with Dr. Lopez to make the proposal.

The beautiful Ingrid, who was buffing her nails, paused to usher Dr. Mendoza, Ms. Wulferson, and María into Dr. Lopez's office, where a first-rate computer was enshrined. It was the first Margaret had seen at the university.

Her duties fulfilled, Ingrid silently exited and Dr. Lopez sat down at the computer to compose the letter to be sent to all the universities in Peru.

"Oh, very good," Dr. Mendoza said, perusing the letter. "But don't you need to include Ms. Wulferson's name?"

"Oh, yes," Dr. Lopez said, making a quick emendation.

Now, sitting at the homey kitchen table, Luis complained that Dr. Lopez had not yet sent out the letters of invitation. The letters stated that the new English class the university was offering began on September 7th.

"And today is September 5th."

"I have just four students left in my class now," Margaret said. "But it's not my responsibility to recruit students. My responsibility is to teach well—one or four or fifteen. If the university wants to pay me for teaching four students, I can't help that."

Margaret spoke passionately, but then she remembered that Luis had once pointed out to her that the way the contract with the university read, the university could say, "Sorry, we don't have enough students to make up a class," and terminate her. Were they trying to drive her away? Once the head of the United States Information Service had asked how her classes were going. She paused before replying. The embassy, after all, was paying half her salary.

"Sometimes I think all I'm doing is providing good will for the United States."

He gave her a knowing look.

"I'm happy with that."

"So could you stay in Peru and return home for a month or two every year?" Luis was asking.

"What?"

"We could create an institute, under the aegis of the university, to prepare students for the Test of English as a Foreign Language. So many Peruvians want to study at American universities. I could teach the first classes, preparing the students for your advanced classes. Just think, it would be the only one in Peru!"

(Yet Margaret had seen storefront institutions in Lima advertising preparation for the TOEFL.)

"How about it?"

"No, I couldn't."

"But think what an outstanding institute we could create, with students coming from all over Peru."

"I said from the first I intended to come for just one year—that's all," Margaret said firmly.

"Then what about a summer institute," he countered, "three months, two or three months during your summer vacation? You could do that, couldn't you?"

Margaret was silent, revolving the idea in her mind. The others, who had been unable to follow the rapid fire conversation in English, asked Luis to explain.

He concluded by saying, "And she said yes."

"No! I said nothing. I'm thinking."

"But why come for a year to teach four students when you could come for two months and teach fifteen?"

"But why are you pressuring her about the future?" Angeles asked. "The real problem is how to increase her current class. All you have to do is put an ad in the paper and you will get plenty of applicants."

"Just think what a success we could have, with your advanced class following my preparatory class!"

"He needs to put an ad in the paper now," Angeles said to María.

"I'll have to think about it," Margaret said.

The gray overcast hung like a pall over the city, over the garbage-strewn sands of the broad median in front of the university, over the big black sixties Chevrolet. Just as Luis pulled onto the thoroughfare, a loud thump emanated from the rear of the car. He slammed on the brakes and leapt out. Behind the car, a man was picking himself up off the ground, his baggy trousers ripped at the groin. He wobbled toward the other side of the street on the arm of another staggering man.

"He's drunk," Luis reported to María and Margaret. "Apparently he fell against the car and his trousers caught on the bumper. When I started up, his pants ripped. Luckily, he wasn't hurt."

The two drunkards, their clothes so ragged and dusty that the torn trousers weren't particularly noticeable, staggered off arm in arm across the barren sand, as Luis drove off.

The neighbors were gathered in front of his home, the door open onto the grimy street, when young Luis came striding down the sidewalk swinging his briefcase. They moved aside and he rushed through the door.

His mother was seated in the small parlor between two neighbor women, tears running down her face.

"Lui, there's been an accident," the next-door neighbor said, putting his arm across Luis's shoulder.

Luis heard his sister's voice in the kitchen. He looked bewildered.

"Your father was drinking and fell in front of a car."

When wasn't he drinking, Luis thought.

"Aren't you stopping at Scala?" María asked from the front seat.

"Yes, certainly," Luis said, startled, and at the last moment turned into the large parking lot. As he pulled into one of the parking spaces, a street vendor ran forward.

"Not there. You're too close to my cart." The vendor indicated the cart full of t-shirts he had rolled from the street onto the Scala parking lot.

Dr. Mendoza backed up, paused, then honked his horn. The vendor looked puzzled. Dr. Mendoza continued honking until the street vendor approached.

María rose up in her seat, inflamed, but before she could speak, Dr. Mendoza said, "Don't say a word."

When the vendor reached the car, Dr. Mendoza motioned to a parking place a few spaces away.

"Is this one all right?"

"Yes."

"You're very kind," Dr. Mendoza said sternly, in a tone of great authority, and pulled into the space.

The vendor was still staring as the three disappeared into Scala, and Luis began to laugh.

María wandered down the aisles of Scala, with its rows and rows of consumer goods like a big American store, enchanted, while Luis gathered the items on Angeles's list. From Scala, he drove the women to their bus stops. On a side street, a wizened man, his lined and weathered face blackened and creased with the grime of the street, sat in a pile of garbage. He was chewing on something he had found in the refuse littering the street, as unselfconscious as a dog.

"Come," Luis said one morning, "We have a meeting with Dr. Olivarez."

Luis drove across the sandy waste down the road leading to the main building. Once again guards unlocked the heavy forbidding doors. María and Margaret followed Luis down the hallway, which functioned as a small gallery of paintings and modern sculpture, to the rector's office. Dr. Olivarez was acting rector for the week, while the rector, who spoke French fluently, attended an international conference in Paris.

Dr. Olivarez stood up from the leather arm chair, the large desk before him dark with the rich patina of age.

"Come in, come in."

He shook hands with all three, motioned toward the leather overstuffed couch and arm chairs.

"Sit down, sit down."

Margaret looked around the room. It was well proportioned, with heavy carved woodwork. Tall windows admitted the gray light of Lima. When Dr. Mendoza and Dr. Olivarez had finished their business, she brought up the matter of her visa renewal. A traveler entering Peru automatically receives a three-months' visa, but she had been told before she left the States how difficult it was to get an extension. Dr. Lopez had already given her the run-around. But without an extension, she could not legally remain in the country.

"My visa expires in a month. Can the university get a renewal?"

"Consider it done." Dr. Olivarez smiled warmly as he shook her hand.

"Dr. Olivarez has invited my son and me to lunch at his house on Saturday, Margaret said one morning. How should my son dress?"

Dr. Olivarez, the rotund vice-rector, Luis's ally, was quite different from the elegant and forbidding rector.

"A blazer and tie would be appropriate," Luis said.

"Jeans and a t-shirt would be fine," María said.

Margaret looked from one to the other.

"It's the home of the vice-rector of the university!" Luis said.

"Yes, but he's a kid."

Dr. Olivarez had said he would pick Margaret and her son up at twelve, but at twelve he called to say he would be late. Two and a half hours later, Dr. Olivarez and his son, Ivan, arrived at the house in Miraflores.

Margaret had leaned towards María's advice, but had hedged by having her son wear a white button-down shirt with his jeans. Ivan had on a crumpled gray-green army fatigue shirt. Her son turned a reproachful glance on Margaret before climbing into the back of the official university vehicle, an old beat-up, double-cab pick-up.

"We had car trouble on the way," Dr. Olivarez said cheerfully. He was wearing slacks and a sport shirt, the buttons tight on his plump body.

The Olivarezes lived in the wealthy suburb of Monterrico, some distance north of Miraflores and even wealthier, with some homes boasting two swimming pools. By the time they reached Monterrico, the pick-up quit running again. This time it was out of gas.

Dr. Olivarez hailed a passing taxi, helped Margaret squeeze into the back seat with the boys, climbed into the front and directed the driver first to a gas station before sending the taxi on with Margaret and the boys.

Señora Olivarez, wearing a simple skirt and blouse, stood on the doorstep and warmly welcomed Ms. Wulferson and her son.

"Papá will be here soon," Ivan said.

The Olivarezes were all dressed informally, in the American style, and indeed they had lived in Texas during the fifties, as had the other couple, the Perezes. Dr. Perez wore a suit and tie, his wife an elegant dress with pearls, according to the more formal Peruvian custom.

"Good afternoon," Dr. Olivarez said genially as he entered, and shook hands all around. Señora Olivarez offered glasses of sherry on a tray, and Dr. Olivarez brought out copies of old UT yearbooks from the years he and Dr. Perez had attended.

"May I remove my jacket?" Dr. Perez asked, before carefully folding it over the back of the couch. Both husband and wife had looked uncomfortable when they saw the attire of their hosts.

At other parties Margaret had so far attended, the guests were dressed as the Perezes were today. At the university, professors wore unobtrusive clothing, slacks and wool sweaters with a tie, even the rector and Dr. Lopez, as though it would be bad form to dress expensively. The university was devoted to a higher calling, the clothing of its members seemed to say, the life of the mind. Its doors were open to the poorer classes, to all who shared the vision. Margaret wondered, however, how many trunks Señora Lopez carried on the European trips Dr. Lopez had alluded to, and how Dr. Lopez himself must dress in social circles outside the university. The Olivarezes, however, seemed to be embracing American chic.

The boys of the family, taking Margaret's son with them, were roaming outdoors; the daughter remained inside with the adults. It was after 4:00 now, and Margaret hoped her rumbling stomach was inaudible. She found a picture of her mother's first cousin in one of the yearbooks and identified it.

"Oh, your uncle," Dr. Perez said.

"No, my mother's cousin."

"Yes, your uncle."

Margaret paused, remembering the strong family ties that bind Peruvians, the intricate web of relationships that governed their lives. The Olivarez family included two sons, a daughter, and a nephew living with them, all of whom were at the table, the nephew indistinguishable from the sons, when finally the group sat down for lunch at 7:00 o'clock at night.

The Perezes drove Margaret and her son back, and this time the trip from the ultra wealthy suburb of Monterrico to the wealthy suburb of Mirafores seemed swift. The city lights glittered, but the darkness underneath concealed the grime and soot of Lima, its inefficiencies and despair.

"Good morning, Margaret," Luis said heartily from his desk at the back of the classroom as she entered through the front of the room. "How was your trip?" He had missed her while she was on vacation.

"Good morning. We had a wonderful time. Where's María?"

"She'll be in later. I know she'll want to hear all about your travels."

"Oh, by the way, Luis, my visa expired two months ago."

"What!" He looked startled, alarmed even. He picked up the phone, but as was so often the case, it didn't work. He stood up abruptly and hurried out of the room without even asking Margaret to accompany him to the main building. By the end of the day, he had a letter from the vice rector and an appointment at the Ministry of Foreign Affairs for the next morning. Margaret smiled to herself as she left for the day.

The next morning, the gates to the university were locked. The workers—the classified employees—were on strike. The notice said the gates would remain locked until 10:00 A.M. The letter from Dr. Olivarez, the vice rector, requesting Margaret's visa extension was in Dr. Mendoza's office. There was nothing they could do but wait.

Margaret remembered her friend Bob telling her how difficult it was to get a visa renewed through official channels—impossible in his case, even though the family who had considered him almost a son had been highly connected. She remembered the run-around Dr. Lopez had given her, sending her to the U.S. Embassy, which had no authority over Peruvian internal affairs.

Finally the gates were unlocked. Luis rushed in to get the letter, sped with Margaret and María out the gates of the university, back across the Rimac River, and down the winding streets of old downtown.

They were over an hour late for the appointment at the Ministry of Foreign Affairs. Luis led the two women up the steps into the old colonial building with its heavy, carved wooden doors. A brief wait, and then they were ushered through the outer offices into the interior office of the minister in charge. A few polite words with the minister, and in ten minutes Margaret had the stamp on her passport that enabled her to remain legally in the country for a full year. Amazed at her own success, she stood bemused on the soot-darkened sidewalk outside.

"Are you coming?" Luis called out to her. He and María stood waiting under the high gray overcast that shrouded all Lima.

Margaret waited in the big black Chevy outside a pharmacy in the Plaza 2 de Mayo while Luis picked up a prescription for María's daughter Lourdes, the one with problems, who was sick once again. Foul smells arose from the pools of stinking water and garbage.

A man spat into a putrid puddle, then blew his nose without a handkerchief and flung his snot after his spit. Next to the effluvia in what would have been the gutter had the street had one rested the lines of vendors' carts. In the shade of one, a woman sat on a low platform on rollers eating her lunch, while another rinsed her plate and spoon in a pail of greasy grey water. An ice cream cart came by and a man bought a cone and began eating it as he walked down the fetid street. Another man bought a banana from one of the carts and ate it there by the stinking pool he dropped the skin into. A school girl in the requisite gray skirt and white blouse sat on a stool in the shade of the awning, reading a magazine, while her father arranged shoes on the cart. A small boy ran laughing down the grimy sidewalk.

Not far from Plaza 2 de Mayo, shacks lined the bank of the Rimac River, a running sewer, home to these vendors, Margaret guessed, their place of business just a step away from their homes, and all of a piece. What must it be like, she thought, to grow up in such surroundings: people laughing, talking, eating, teasing, reading, passing the time of day, oblivious to the foul-smelling, pestilent ugliness of their surroundings.

"They had it," Luis said enthusiastically. He climbed into the car without a glance at the reeking plaza, happy to have found the medicine María needed for Lourdes.

"Do you want to see the procession of Our Lord of Miracles?" Luis asked one day.

In one of Lima's churches hangs a large picture of Christ which miraculously survived an earthquake over 300 years ago. Ever since then the painting of Our Lord of Miracles has been brought forth from the church on two days in October and carried on a litter through the downtown streets.

"When El Señor de los Milagros arrives at the Plaza de Armas, the President comes out of the palace to kneel down and kiss Him," María said.

Margaret wanted to see the procession, so Luis drove them downtown, parking west of Avenida Woodrow Wilson, many blocks away from the route of the procession. The crowded downtown streets were even more densely crowded on this grey spring day. Fewer buses fouled the air with their black exhaust, but vendors with trays of food—greasy meats and wilted vegetables, sweet pastries attracting flies—clotted the streets.

"You want to die tomorrow?" Luis said, nodding toward the food.

The crowd grew thicker the farther they walked until the street was a single mass of people.

"I'll wait here," María said, taking shelter on a side street.

"You don't want to come?" Margaret asked, surprised.

María shook her head.

"She's claustrophobic," Luis said softly.

Struggling through the crowd, Luis and Margaret finally came to the street on the painting's route. It seemed all the narrow streets of old Lima were funneling the population of the city to its center, where El Señor was making his slow progress. From building front to building front, the sidewalks and street directly in the path of the procession were a solid mass of people. Luis and Margaret stood at the intersection of a side street and the processional street. Luis was explaining to Margaret the route of the procession when from that direction people ran yelling for an ambulance, forcing a path through the crowd for a man carrying a toddler who had fainted.

Behind them, the side street filled until they were completely enclosed by the massing crowd.

"Look! There He is, there He is!" Luis pointed toward the painting of Christ a block away carried on a litter above the sea of heads.

The flood of people, filling the streets as far as the eye could see, became more and more densely packed as the crowd surged forward in anticipation. As though parting the waters, the procession inched its way forward, its progress infinitesimal, measured not by sight—it seemed to be in essentially the same place—but by the wavelike movement of people crushed against each other.

The crowd was so densely packed it didn't seem possible for anything or anyone to move, yet still the procession continued, and the succession of waves grew stronger and more frequent.

It was now impossible to leave, even to move, had anyone wanted to.

As the painting, visible above the heads of the crowd, bobbed ever closer, with each wave it became more and more difficult for Margaret to keep her footing. Bodies squeezed against her, cutting off her breath and threatening her balance.

Though crushed into the mass of humanity beside her, Luis stood solid, immovable.

As each rippling movement gathered force, crushing people more and more tightly together, one could hear people gasping, as though they could hardly breathe. When the crest passed, there would be a collective, inaudible sigh. Then the wave would come again.

"There He comes," Luis said excitedly.

Gradually, riding on waves, each wave compressing them until they could hardly breathe, the procession came abreast of Luis and Margaret. Over the tops of people's heads, as they stood part of the congealed mass of bodies, they could see the painting in its heavy gilt frame, weighted down with additional gold and silver donated by the faithful. At the four corners of the litter, tall twisted candleholders of heavy ornate silver supported huge candles. The bearers, in flowing purple robes, clung solemnly to the litter poles. Each compression, each one fiercer than the last, seemed to fuse the endless crowd into a single panting entity.

Margaret fought down a moment of panic. She couldn't breathe. She was terrified of falling beneath the feet of the massive crowd. A single entity, enormous, pulsating. She clenched her teeth, willed herself to stay upright as the last, unbelievable compression of the ultimate wave swept into her. Her mind went blank, and all that was left was the tactile sense: being crushed, without breath. Time ceased to exist.

Luis stood stolid beside her.

Then, as the procession inched its way past them, the waves gradually decreased in intensity, finally subsiding altogether, until the crowd thinned enough for Luis to move. Margaret stood stunned.

"This way," Luis said, then paused reverently. "This is the first time I have ever seen Him—outside of the church."

Young Lui stood outside the church. The dark cool interior both beckoned and frightened him. He squared his strong broad shoulders and started up the stone steps. The familiar scent of incense comforted him as he forced himself to take each step.

Inside the confessional booth he began: "Father, I have sinned. I have raised my hand against my father."

Lui strode down the sidewalk, book bag slung over his broad shoulders, beaming. He couldn't wait to tell his mother. He had won first prize for his English essay and had been warmly commended by the principal himself.

He was whistling to himself as he bounded through the door into the dimly lighted kitchen. His mother was cowering against the stove, her arms up to protect her face.

His father was leaning over her, a cast iron skillet in his hand, raised to strike.

Without thinking, Luis leapt forward and grabbed his father's arm.

"Leave her alone!"

His father wheeled around, jerking his arm from Luis's grasp, eyes red with fury.

"Who do you think you are? This is my wife." He swung the skillet at Luis's head, his face twisted with rage.

Luis moved forward, into the whiskey stink of his father's breath, inside the skillet's trajectory, almost embracing his father. The blow, its force broken, landed on the back of his right shoulder. It hurt like hell.

He swung as hard as he could with his left fist, hitting his father's belly.

His father gasped, then roared and tried to swing the skillet again. Luis slammed him against the counter, cracked his arm against the stove until the skillet fell from his grasp and landed on Luis's toes. The pain paralyzed him.

His father jammed an elbow into Luis's ribs, and when Luis folded over, ground a knuckle into his eye.

With a roar, Luis threw his father to the floor. He landed on top and grabbed his throat.

Underneath him, his father was bucking and trying to pry his fingers loose. Luis ground a knee into his stomach and leaned hard into the throat. His fingers tightened harder and harder the more fiercely his father struggled.

All those years of his father's drunken rages, beating his mother, lying in a drunken stupor while his mother went out with her vendor's cart, stealing her money to buy whiskey while the family went hungry.

His father's face was red and mottled, turning purple. Gradually he stilled.

"Lui! Lui!" His mother was shouting and pulling on his shoulder.

Her voice seemed to come from far away.

"Lui! Don't kill him, Lui!"

Luis saw the stove in front of him, the gray concrete floor, his father's stilled body beneath him. Dazed, he let go of the grimy throat. He staggered to his feet.

His mother was down on her knees.

"He's breathing."

By the grace of God, he hadn't killed him. He was not a parricide, thanks be to God. Sometimes it took Christ in His processional to remind one of divine intervention. Luis wanted to kneel down on the hard dirty grey pavement under the sombre grey sky and give thanks. Instead, he paused, silent, then turned off down the side street, Margaret walking quietly by his side, until they found María waiting for them.

Luis lies in the small iron-framed bed in a hospital room narrow as a cell. A slender vase holding white irises sits on a small wooden table next to the bed, a glass of thickened water beside it. Memories—pictures—float through his mind.

Angeles that last year not even knowing who he was. His sister, silently sweeping, unmoved. The morning when he found Angeles stiffened and cold, and called the ambulance, knowing but refusing to believe it was too late.

"Look to him!" one of the medics called out.

Falling, falling, but unable to cry out. Hearing the chorus of voices as the young medic caught him enough to break his fall. Staring, unable to move or speak.

Now the hush of the hospital unbroken, week after week, month after month, except by the rustle of a nun's habit or a soft-spoken word as she spoons pureed food into his twisted mouth and half runs down his chin.

All those years in an unbroken pattern. Teaching English to budding engineers. For them, merely a means to an end. An outlier to the real business and glory of the university. Always the same round of chores, the same rung on the ladder. (Still, how he missed it.) Never his own language school, always merely tolerated for his expertise. Where had all the years gone?

The year Margaret came—like a spurt of flame, the brief flash before the fire dies down.

"My prince," his mother had said one final time, her hand resting on his head in benediction. He knelt on the floor, his face against the red and black counterpane, racked with sobs.

The grey light of Lima, oppressed by the perpetual shroud of fog, barely illuminates the room. In the distance, the cold steel-colored sea laps against the grey shores of the city, the high overcast shadowing the intricate maze of the city, the people caught in invisible webs of their own making.

Noises at the door. María and his goddaughter Teresa enter, their visitor faces slowly transformed into shock. They stand frozen just inside the room.

Luis struggles violently to communicate, but the only outward sign is the burning intensity of his eyes.

"María! Teresa!" his mind screams as they flee out the door, back underneath the grey vault of Lima's sky, the grey light that barely fills the room.

Angela

When Margaret, her class finished for the day, strolled down the iron walkway with her son, Dr. Mendoza and María were outside his office talking to a middle-aged woman with bleached blonde hair. A pale high overcast had turned the sky, functional campus buildings, all Lima colorless.

"Angie is going your way and has offered to give you and your son a ride to Miraflores," Dr. Mendoza said after introductions were completed.

The group stepped down the iron stairs from the Language Arts Center to the broad sandy waste below. A tall yellow hibiscus and a little red rose bush bloomed behind a border of multicolored marigolds in the carefully watered plot by the metal stairs, giving a touch of color to the drab landscape. Canals disposing of chemicals from the science complex provided the only other color in the wide stretches of barren sand. Today they ran red.

"You can climb over the gear shift from the driver's side or I can unwire the passenger door for you to get in," Angie explained as the group approached her car.

Margaret's son, who was still accompanying her to the university, clambered over the driver's seat and gear shift into the back seat of the solid 1960s two-door sedan, once an indeterminate shade of green, now faded with age; then Margaret crawled over the shift into the front passenger seat. Both were grateful for what would be a half-hour drive across the city instead of an hour or more of standing wearily, crushed and jostled in the crowded bus aisles.

Angie was a skilled driver, maneuvering through crowded streets faster than Margaret would have taken them, but with a subtle constant awareness. She was just a few years older than Margaret, but her skin, fairer than María's, was coarse, with fine lines near the eyes.

Today the endless high fog over Lima that turned the city grey pressed down on Margaret harder than usual. Vendors' carts covered the garbage-strewn sidewalks, threatening to spill over onto the dirty grey pavement of the streets, and the pale muted light covered all. Angie, though, was in high spirits, chatting gaily as she drove. One of Angela's three grown sons lived in Hawaii, and she was now sitting in on one of Dr. Mendoza's classes, determined to learn English. Like so many other Peruvians, she hoped to live in the States. Unlike most Peruvian women, although in straitened circumstances, she had a car and sold real estate.

Margaret put aside her worries about her students and gave herself over to the moment. Angie was different from the other women Margaret had met in heavily Catholic Peru, with its clear delineation of the ideals of womanhood. María, still loving and faithful to the husband who had abandoned her years ago, struggled against the odds to provide for their eight daughters, uncomplaining. Margaret often had to bite her tongue. The most impressive of her Peruvian friends confided that her husband had also left her many years ago for another woman. Though in her sixties now, Helga too was waiting for the day he would return. Helga, however, a remnant of the oligarchy, was wealthy and quite comfortable. Her servant provided a constant stream of mundane details of her husband's everyday life, gleaned from one of her husband's many servants. Margaret's landlady, Yolanda, was almost a caricature of a bourgeoise, the power in the house, with an eye to the cost of everything. Angie, though with the signs of hard living in her face, seemed a free spirit.

As she drove down one of the major thoroughfares, Angie suddenly said, "Excuse me a moment, but I need to change some money," and pulled off onto a small side street.

Margaret had learned that there were many places around the city where dollars could be exchanged for intis, so she looked for the sign, Cambio, that indicates a money exchange house.

Suddenly strange men in the narrow street were rushing up to the side of the car, yelling.

"No, no, no!" Angie cried.

Their voices raised, the men shouted over one another as they swarmed the car.

At first Margaret couldn't distinguish words in the babble of voices of the frantically gesticulating men.

Her son sat still and silent in the back seat, watching.

Then Angie said, "Thirty-six."

"Thirty-one," a man shouted back, racing alongside the car.

"No, no, no!" Angie yelled, speeding up and looking straight ahead.

One enterprising young man grabbed hold of the vent bar and at a dead run kept up with the car, shouting out figures.

Angie pressed down on the accelerator, stared straight ahead, and shouted back.

"Thirty-five," she insisted.

She raced down the narrow street.

"Thirty-three," he yelled, his hand locked to the vent bar as he sprinted to keep alongside the speeding car.

The shouting of numbers continued until the sprinter, holding on for dear life, finally weakened.

"Thirty-four," he said.

Angie smiled and stopped the car. She pulled out a $20 bill, asked if he had that many intis. He pulled out a calculator and told her how many intis at 34 intis to the dollar that was. Then Angie took the calculator from him to do her own calculations. Satisfied, she was about to complete the deal.

By this time, however, she was stopped at a stoplight that had changed and angry horns were honking behind her. Angie handed the man his calculator and motioned to him to meet us farther up the street. The young man ran the half a block, pulled out his intis, and took her twenty dollars.

Margaret turned toward the back seat, and she and her son stared at each other. Angie merely pulled back onto a main artery and continued whatever discussion had been interrupted by a bit of business.

* * *

On days when Angie came to the university and didn't have an appointment afterwards, she gave rides to Margaret and María.

"Tell me," she said one day in Spanish as they were speeding down Avenida Garciloso de la Vega, "what is the dirtiest word in English."

One of the shabby yellow buses ahead of them had stopped to pick up a line of people patiently waiting on the grey pavement: small tired men in stained and work torn clothes; a time and weather worn campesina with long dark braids hanging down her back, wearing a long black skirt, a once white blouse, and a tall black hat, with a brightly colored blanket slung across her shoulders; a young heavily pregnant mother holding a round-faced, black-eyed toddler by the hand; two middle-aged women with shopping bags standing together and gossiping.

A large green bus carrying mostly professionals sped around the smaller yellow one, belching black plumes of exhaust.

Angie had half turned toward Margaret in the back seat to ask her question.

Margaret thought for a moment, unnerved by Angie's momentarily taking her eyes off the busy street.

"Fuck," she said after some consideration, as Angie turned back and whipped around the shabby yellow bus.

Angie smiled and filed the word away.

In the front seat, María made no comment.

* * *

Over coffee one day the three women discussed men, Margaret in her halting Spanish, Angie contributing the few English words she had learned, María relying on her intuition to bridge the gaps in Margaret's Spanish. Margaret had invited the other two, which meant that she was hosting the coffee. They sat at a small rickety table in the dusty adobe cafe built on the wide sands of the university campus, waited on by the ageless Indian proprietor, one of the many campesinos who had left the high Andes to try their luck in the coastal capital.

"Peruvian men are more romantic than Anglos," Margaret ventured.

"Yes, but it is a false romanticism," Angie said. A momentary shadow passed across her face. She confided that her long-time boyfriend had recently left her for a younger woman. She did not speak of her husband's having kicked her out of the house to make room for his mistress, leaving her to survive as best she might. It was a long time ago.

María was silent.

Margaret tried again. "Your middle son lives in Hawaii?"

"Yes, he has started an export/import business. I plan to join him there some day."

A sparkle had returned to Angie's eyes.

"And your other two sons?"

"My oldest son works for a company here in Lima. My youngest, the one with problems, lives with his father. I see him once a week."

"This coffee is really good." María took a last sip. "We often come here with Dr. Mendoza," she said, turning to Angie, "but he was not well today."

"Thank you for the coffee," Angie said to Margaret, "but I have an appointment coming up. I can take you both as far as Plaza 2 de Mayo."

The proprietor, whose dusky skin was the color of the adobe bricks that she and her family had made of mud and straw on site when they built this modest cafe, silently removed the empty cups from their table.

* * *

When the phone rang downstairs, Margaret was deep in concentration at the desk she and her son shared in their room. Señora Yolanda came bustling up the stairs to get her.

"I would like to invite you to Angela's birthday party," Angie's sister said, and gave Margaret the address in Barranco, a suburb adjacent to Miraflores on the south.

Margaret was unsure whether the invitation included her son, but in any case he chose to stay home so he could do all his school work for the next day.

Once the city's seaside resort, Barranco was now a kind of Limeño Greenwich Village, Margaret had been told, with artists and young intellectuals taking over many of the older properties.

"Where is your son?" Angie asked as soon as Margaret entered the second floor apartment. Its high ceilings and large archway between living room and an alcove containing a battered upright piano were from another era.

"He had homework to finish."

Angie's sister gave her son a significant look.

"You see," she said quietly to him.

"My house is your house," said her husband, Angie's brother-in-law. "Whatever you need during your stay in Lima, just ask for it. I will be happy to provide whatever you desire."

In the flurry of introductions, Margaret ascertained that one man was an engineer, one woman worked for a company that imports oil equipment from the United States, Angie's sister was a stay-at-home mother.

"She's the intelligent one," Angie said, putting her arm around her sister, "but she's not using her intelligence."

The son, Angie's 16-year-old nephew, led Margaret around the apartment. To Margaret, it was reminiscent of a graduate student apartment, but with evidence of much more money. The children had a very large color television in their room, such as she had not yet seen elsewhere. Helga, scion of a sugar plantation oligarch, had a small unobtrusive black and white one. Yolanda, Margaret's landlady, had two black and white TVs of modest size, one in her bedroom and one downstairs in the kitchen.

On the wall in the living room was a print entitled Old New Orleans. Another was quite 19th century romantic: Greek ruins with broken columns, the figure of a young woman in a supplicating attitude. In the dining room, a plume arrangement in a vase sat in the center of a long cloth covered table, a Last Supper on the wall above it.

Leo, the son, ended the tour at the alcove, where he immediately sat down at the piano and rattled off a lively piece. He played well, though obviously self-taught, but the piano was jarringly out of tune.

"Pisco sour," Angie's sister offered, holding out the cocktail, "or would you prefer a beer?"

Margaret happily accepted the pisco sour. Some of the company were dancing to the beat of salsa music while others stood talking. When Angie took the floor, most people turned to watch. In a society of excellent dancers, Angie was outstanding, full of life and grace.

"Isn't she good," people murmured admiringly.

"Which birthday is it?" someone called out as Angie twirled around the floor.

"My fifteenth," she responded archly, as though celebrating her quinceanera.

From time to time Angie and her sister retreated to the kitchen to make yet another batch of pisco sours, and beer, iced in tubs, was plentiful. A chicken and rice dish slowly simmered on the stove.

Most of the guests spoke some English, and many were fluent. Angie introduced Margaret to a man who had lived in New York City for some time. Now back in Lima and troubled with arthritis, he had been consulting a Polish doctor.

"Many years ago this doctor ventured into the jungles of the Amazon Basin," he began in fluent English. "He became so fascinated with the vast medical knowledge of the indigenous people that he remained and has been studying with their herbalists for twenty years. He comes back to Lima for a few months every year to treat patients, then returns to the jungle to continue his apprenticeship.

"As long as I stay on the diet and herbal regimen, I don't have any problems. But the doctor said I had consulted him just in time, for a little later the arthritis would have reached the irreversible stage."

"Another pisco sour?" Angie said, proffering glasses. Margaret accepted, while her new acquaintance declined.

By this time the party had become quite lively. Margaret had not seen this much drinking so far in Peru. When Helga had given a party for her, attended by a small but distinguished group—a diplomat and his wife, a young film maker studying in London, a writer, an international businessman and his wife—there had of course been liquor served. But like so much of the ceremony of Peruvian life, it was ritualized: a drink before dinner, wine with the meal. Wide-ranging, thoughtful conversation was the main event. This party was much more like a hard-drinking American one, at least in its consumption of alcohol.

Aromas from the kitchen had become more and more enticing the later it grew. Finally, plates of chicken and rice were served, a coda to the evening, and afterwards Angie, full of lively conversation about the party, drove Margaret home through the dark, silent streets of Lima.

* * *

One day in late August, still winter in Lima, where winter means temperatures in the sixties under a colorless sky, María and Margaret were invited to a party at Angie's apartment.

"It's very small," Angie said apologetically.

María and Margaret climbed a spiral iron staircase that led to the flat roof of a once grand home, now divided into apartments. Angie had the whole open rooftop of the house as her living room, yard, patio. In one corner was a small bedroom and bath and a roofed but otherwise open cooking area: formerly the maid's quarters, but no one was tactless enough to comment on it.

It was one of those rare days when the garua, the persistent high fog that looms over Lima in the winter, had lifted, along with everyone's spirits.

"This is Victor," Angie said, introducing a slender suave man. "He makes documentaries. And this is Juan."

Juan was an older man, with large bulbous features and coarsened skin.

Two heavily made-up women with bleached hair stood together and were not introduced. María glanced at them and moved closer to Margaret. Her gaze taking in the whole party, she whispered: "It's a good thing we brought no children."

Angie put on a salsa tape and Juan, the coarse-featured older man, moved in next to the two women and asked Margaret to dance. Afterwards, he tried to beguile her with references to his impressive business deals.

A clattering on the spiral iron stair case announced the arrival of Fernando, a fresh-faced young man. At six feet, large and lean, he was extremely tall for a Peruvian, more reminiscent of an athletic American youth. He seemed out of place in this group. Unlike Juan, who kept urging Margaret to let him take her home, and Victor, who was pressuring her to promise she would call him at his office, Fernando seemed genuinely open and kind. María gravitated to him at once. She spoke earnestly with him, her dark eyes warm and serious. Soon they were dancing.

Angie flitted among her guests, making sure everyone had a full drink and passing around individual cigarettes from a fresh pack, her worn face lighted up and the coarsened skin softened by the dim light. Drink in hand, cigarette poised between two fingers, María danced in sinuous grace to the insistent beat of salsa under the revealed stars.

Below the dancers, Lima lay quiescent in the gathering dusk.

Angie passed by, and Margaret accepted yet another pisco sour. She felt like tossing it back. The relentless pursuit of Victor and Juan had become extremely tiresome. If she were to accept their earnest requests to go out, she knew she would spend the entire evening fighting them off. Only because she was studying another culture, she decided, the party wasn't a complete waste of time.

Suddenly it struck her that this was the demimonde, and Peru a culture still capable of making such distinctions. She remembered how immediately suspicious of Angie her oppressively middle-class landlady had been, while recognizing María's respectability at first glance.

Overhead the stars shone in a dark clear sky as María and Margaret took their leave. Angie kissed them on both cheeks, thanked them for coming, and floated off to her other guests, her spirit seemingly untouched by the world she inhabited.

* * *

Angie parked the ancient faded green Packard sedan, a basic model with a heavy steel frame, its occasional dents mere dimples, near the large house, set back from the street, that had once been hers. A small magnolia tree with creamy white blossoms grew in the front corner of the immaculately clipped lawn. The two poinsettia trees on either corner at the front of the house now reached almost to the bottom of the top floor, their red leaves vivid above the greenery below.

The drive was now bordered with pale orange and yellow Lillies of the Inca. She paused to stare with admiration at them, then continued down the curving gravel drive to the back of the house and entered through the kitchen. It was mid-afternoon, a time when the staff would be taking a break. All was still and quiet now in this part of the house.

Copper-bottomed pots hung gleaming above the stove. Garlic, onions, and purple potatoes hung in a triple layered wire basket, each in its own basket of ascending size. From the same beam hung a string of bright red peppers. On open shelves she saw the blue and white pottery dishes she had once used for everyday. A brand new red blender sat on the polished wooden counter.

Angie walked down the long, familiar corridor to a large airy bedroom near the front of the house. The grey light from an open window at the head of the bed filled the room and brightened the red and brown striped spread. From the thick shrubbery outside came the mournful cry of a dove.

"Miguel!"

"Mamá."

She reached out and took him in her arms, though he towered over her. He was dressed in grey slacks and a light blue sweater, his loafers highly polished, and he was well groomed, though his hair was a little rumpled as though he had been lying on that side.

"How have you been, Miguel?"

It had been a week since she had last seen him, in accordance with the terms her husband had laid down.

Miguel looked vacant, but smiled when Angie patted his arm. He had a comfortable brown couch in his spacious bedroom, and Angie sat down with him there.

Against the opposite wall, a half-finished tower sat among a pile of legos on a small table. A poster of Machu

Picchu hung on that wall, though Miguel had never been there. Now that Americans and Europeans were flocking to the site, it had recently become quite fashionable. On the wall above them hung a Daumier print of Don Quixote on Rocinante, with Sancho Panza a blur in the background.

Angie took Miguel's hand and began to talk about his brother in Hawaii.

"You haven't forgotten him, have you?" and when he didn't respond, "Gustavo. You remember Gustavo, your brother Gustavo, don't you?"

There was a flicker of recognition in Miguel's eyes, and Angie began to describe Gustavo's house near the beach, where the white-capped waves of a brilliant blue ocean rolled up on a white sand beach and the gulls cried overhead. She spoke of how Gustavo was working to build a thriving export/import business in Hawaii, how he had fallen in love with the island and its people, how she planned to visit him someday. She held Miguel's hand as she talked, and her voice was soothing.

After a while, she glanced at her watch.

"I must be going now, but I'll be back soon."

She stroked his hand. Miguel stood up when she did, and reached out to hug her and be hugged.

Angie stumbled on the way out, almost missing the step, her eyes filled with tears.

* * *

"I'm leaving!" Angie said one day, bouncing up the iron steps to the Language Center and entering the classroom. Dr. Mendoza was behind his desk, his work finished for the day, and Margaret was seated on a chair just in front and to the side of his desk. María was straightening up the language lab, with its sixties large-reel tapes—her domain—while they waited for her to finish.

Dr. Mendoza looked blank.

"I sold my car and bought a ticket to Hawaii."

"Oh my," Dr. Mendoza said.

"That's wonderful!" Margaret said, leaping up.

María dropped the earphones she was holding and crossed to the classroom side of the room. She looked shocked.

"But your studies . . ." Dr. Mendoza began.

"Oh, I don't have to know that much English. I'll be living with my son. And in the stores . . ." Laughing, eyes sparkling, she mimed pointing with her index finger at an item and counting up cost with her other fingers.

María was silent.

Dr. Mendoza looked stunned.

"We have to celebrate," Margaret said.

"Oh, of course," Dr. Mendoza said, rallying. "Let's have pie and coffee."

The three clanged down the iron stairs and crossed the pale powdery fine sand to Dr. Mendoza's big black sixties Chevy. From the front passenger seat, María glanced back at Angie as though she had never really quite seen her before. Dr. Mendoza drove a quarter mile down the sandy track to their favorite little adobe cafe on campus. On the way they passed the caretaker's grounds, solitary in the middle of the barren sands of the campus: a simple adobe house with a stand of tall corn growing by its side and rust-colored chickens scratching in the dirt. A little boy with smudges on his face was playing in the sand with a tan dog of uncertain origin.

Around the rickety wooden table in the dim interior of the dusky cafe, whose only light came from the open door, Dr. Mendoza, María, and Margaret saluted Angie, each in turn.

"How exciting to begin a new life in a new country," Margaret said. "Hawaii is beautiful."

"May your reunion with your son be wonderful and your new life be filled with blessings," Dr. Mendoza said. "But don't forget your friends, who will miss you and think of you always."

"To your new life and the reunion with your dear son, whom I know you have missed so much. It will be a happy time, a beautiful time, but we will miss you. You must send us postcards and tell us all about it," María said.

Angie smiled, but tears gathered in her eyes. She was joining one son, whom she had missed terribly, but she was leaving two behind. It was true that Jorge, her oldest, shunned her, turning a cold eye on her and standing with his father. But Miguel, her baby, the one with problems, would she ever see him again? I won't think about that, she said to herself. Who can know the future?

"Thank you, my friends. I will never forget you. When I stand on the sandy beach in Honolulu, I will think of my friends in Lima. And when you stand on the rocky Lima shore and the sea courses over the stones, making that haunting sound, it will be me calling to you from all the way across the Pacific."

Dr. Mendoza looked pleased.

"How beautiful!" María said.

* * *

Angie spent the night before her departure at her sister's apartment. They sat on the couch in the living room beneath the print of the young woman, her back to the viewer, half reclining with her arms stretched out beseechingly, alone among the broken columns of Greek ruins.

They cried together.

"Think how wonderful it will be for you to visit me in Hawaii. I will send you beautiful postcards until you can't bear not to come."

Her sister cried a little more, but finally smiled.

Like most Peruvian women, Angie's sister couldn't drive and had to depend on the men in her family. Her husband was out of town at a conference, so Dr. Mendoza had offered to drive Angie to the airport. He and María picked up Angie and her sister in Barranco. As they left Barranco and traveled north to the suburb of Miraflores, Angie chattered nervously.

Margaret was waiting in the front living room when Dr. Mendoza pressed the intercom buzzer. Adelia, the young servant of all work, pressed the automatic release that admitted him into the courtyard, then undid each of the triple locks, so Dr. Mendoza could escort Margaret to the car. All were comfortably ensconced in the commodious black Chevy, María in the front passenger seat, Margaret, Angie, and Angie's sister comfortably in back, luggage in the spacious trunk.

They drove down Avenida Benavides, past small meticulously tended yards and varnished garage doors inset into high stone walls, walls surmounted by jagged broken glass that protected the triple locked homes behind them. Expensive homes that no doubt were as beautiful and well kept inside as the one Margaret now lived in, with its parquet floors, formal and informal living rooms, formal dining room and everyday kitchen table, colorful tiled bathrooms, all kept to a high polish. The houses had flat roofs (for it never rains in Lima), with rudimentary living quarters for the maid on top—carefully isolated from the family, but with a grand view. The houses were individualized and beautifully kept, but their flat roofs and high protective walls created a fatiguing sameness.

So different from the decayed but elegantly designed El Centro, Margaret thought, with its circular plazas radiating streets. In the sweep of Avenida Ugarte that joined two of the plazas, each with its colonial buildings uniform in size and color (fading orange for one, yellow the other), vestiges remained of the grandeur of the Lima once reputed the most beautiful city in South America. Margaret had been appalled by the filth and danger of the Plaza 2 de Mayo, but she could imagine grand carriages drawn by fine and spirited horses trotting down the avenue, the median filled with bright tropical flowers. Or overlooking the narrow downtown streets, a señorita leaning against the delicate iron grillwork of a balcony to catch a glimpse of her sweetheart among the jostling crowd below before being scolded inside by her duenna.

But contemporary Miraflores, she thought, was closed off from the communal life. Each home, beautifully elegant inside, was a fortress walled off from the life outside: mine, all mine.

Angie, in the middle between her sister and Margaret, was unseeing. As they traversed the streets of Miraflores, her worn face grew taut and the fine lines near her eyes more visible. She held tight to her sister's hand and talked incessantly of nothing.

When they left Miraflores, headed west, Angie suddenly grew silent and her eyes filled. They traveled down the drab and dirty Avenida de la Marina, Angie's sister clutching her hand. The wind swirled a few pieces of trash across the roadway: a torn envelope, a crumpled newspaper, a greasy wrapper. Sky, road, and industrial buildings were dirty grey, the sun a pale diffused ghost behind the garua, the high Lima fog.

At the airport, security allowed the whole group inside the boarding area, for in Peru it would be unthinkable to separate family and close friends from something so traumatic as a leave-taking. Angie and her sister clung to each other, sobbing now. Dr. Mendoza, María, and Margaret sat down together and were silent. Soon Angie and her sister joined them.

"Beautiful Hawaii," María said, and underneath the encouraging tone lay a hint of wistfulness.

"What a wonderful adventure." This from Margaret, herself an adventurer.

Dr. Mendoza sat silent a moment, then said, "Your son will be so happy to see you." His face softened as he imagined the embrace of mother and son.

At boarding time, Angie leapt to her feet, embraced them all, and looked back smiling as she disappeared down the passage to the plane.

Margaret thought they would leave now, but the others returned to their seats. She covered her faux pas by pacing around a few steps before circling back to her seat. They sat solemnly until finally the plane taxied down the runway, roared off into the sky and then disappeared. No one said much as they exited the airport and returned to the big black Chevy.

* * *

Angie found her place, a window seat on the left side of the aisle. A young man in hiking boots and shorts stood up to let her pass.

As the plane taxied down the runway and picked up speed for lift-off, Angie crossed herself, then sent up a quick prayer for the safety of the passengers and crew. She remained tense and still, eyes closed, until the plane reached altitude and cruising speed. Then she looked out the window, but a solid bank of cloud obscured the view below. Angie looked around at her fellow passengers. Many were North Americans, some no doubt fresh from hiking the Inca Trail, like the young man seated next to her. Some of the passengers were Peruvian, perhaps on their way to visit relatives in the States. Or perhaps like Angie herself, heading to a new life.

I have to focus on that, she thought, and began to imagine the beautiful tropical isle, so exotic in her imagination, with its white sand framed by tall palms, bright sun shining on crystalline blue waters. She could almost see the whitecaps, hear the rolling surf as it gently washed against the shore, with nearby the thriving, exciting city of Honolulu.

Not like the sad pale ghost on the Pacific, with its dirty streets crowded with vendors and beggars simply trying to survive. The city where she had lost her oldest son to her hard unyielding husband, the man who had tossed her aside, then scorned her for what she had had to do to survive, who had passed that scorn on to Jorge, her eldest. For a moment a montage of scenes from his babyhood through adolescence passed before her: the beautiful healthy dark-eyed baby, her first-born, whom she suckled so tenderly at her breast; the round-cheeked toddler who laughed with joy and threw his arms around her; the active inquisitive boy, with all his various collections; the handsome adolescent venturing out into the larger world. The distant man who was coldly polite to her.

Angie brushed the tears from her eyes and quickly looked around. The stewardesses were slowly rolling a cart of drinks and snacks down the aisle. A ten-year-old Peruvian boy snapped his fingers at them with an air of imperious command: he had forgotten something he wanted after they had passed.

"I have to think about Gustavo," she said to herself. The son who had left all that behind, who had invited her to come live with him, like a good Peruvian son caring for the mother who wasn't so young anymore. She teared up again thinking of the reunion with him, but this time they were happy tears. She pictured Gustavo standing, waiting with arms outstretched for her.

She half turned, hearing a small commotion a few rows behind her. A momentary flutter of fear distracted her, but it was just a middle-aged man trying to make his way to the aisle past a mountain of a woman overflowing the seat.

So many North Americans were grossly overweight, she thought. So different from Peru, where a large part of the population were struggling just to get enough to eat, where the standard humorous comment among those just above the poverty line, when someone yawned was, "Have you not eaten?" A smile crossed her face as she thought about María, who complained that whenever she lost a few pounds, the men quit giving her admiring glances.

But why did these North Americans get like that, she wondered. Was it some metabolic problem they were born with?

Miguel, my baby! The little child who took so long to learn to walk, but always held out his arms to Mamá, who was happy just sitting in her lap or snuggling next to her on the sofa, who grew up straight and tall, but still with problems. Would he miss her or would he eventually forget her? Angie stifled a sob. Gustavo would always give his brother a home, but her husband would never let Miguel go. He loved his sons, and Miguel was well cared for. Angie took comfort in that, but . . .

Angie looked around the plane. The young man next to her was reading a manual. Across the aisle a young woman was deep into a novel. Others were dozing or talking quietly with the people next to them. A man stared out the window. A Peruvian woman was gently rocking her toddler son in her lap. A stewardess pushing the cart took drink orders.

Angie looked out the window. The plane still soared high above the solid bank of white cloud, the sea below unseen.

The cart rattled to a stop at her row.

Angie turned away from the viewless window.

"A double Scotch," she said.

Brazilian Moon

After the unbroken roar of the boat motor all afternoon, the silence was startling. A faint sound of frogs in the distance. Nearby, the lone call of a night bird and the occasional response of one of its own kind. Above the dark water and the smooth sand, the Big Dipper, upside down, poured out an invisible stream of blackness just above the line of dark forest.

The water lapped quietly against the side of the seventeen meter boat anchored next to the small beach. Under a half moon, the Purus flowed softly, its quiet journey to the far distant Solomões broken only by the occasional plash of a cayman sliding off a log.

Laura sat in the back of the boat, gazing at the dark jungle. In front the young couple, graduate students, practiced their Portuguese with the captain, whose face still reflected astonishment that three gringros were traveling upriver in his boat, their hammocks strung next to the crew's above the cargo of cooking oil, salt, sugar, and diesel.

The trip had begun in Iquitos, Peru, (or it had begun in a child's imagination forty years ago; or it had begun in that invisible stream above/below/beyond the surface).

Laura leans against the balustrade dividing the plaza from the Amazon. Below, in the early morning light, a woman sits on a bench on her rotting, thatch-roofed houseboat, holding a baby who points and coos at the new world. Nearby, three men sit idly on the deck of the Chosen Vessel. A pequepeque piled high with bananas putters past the houseboats, a child steadily bailing with a red pail. The baby toys with its mother's blouse as it suckles.

Laura's breasts ache for the children she never had. And the image reappears: sprawled on the floor, cradling David's head against her breast.

She turns abruptly and walks the length of the plaza.

Mid-morning on the malecón, she sees a man with no legs past the knee, whose arms end at the elbow, sitting in the middle of a circle of dancing people. He, too, dances to the loud music—by bouncing his trunk vigorously up and down on the pavement.

Next morning, a fast boat from Iquitos to Tabatinga skims over the Amazon, brown and smooth, so that floating debris—logs and leafy branches—appear to be lying motionless on top of water dappled by rain drops. Laura and the other passengers breakfast on papaya juice, large tamales with black olives, and sweet hot café con leche. Laura stares across endless water, silent.

Tabatinga, Brazil. Sunday. Buzzards circling overhead, the cry of a black-fronted nun bird. Part of a rainbow stretches across the mounting afternoon clouds hanging above a cluster of palm trees. Laura and the two students need exit stamps for their documents, but the offices across the river are closed.

Two days later, documents stamped, the three sit in a wharf restaurant in Benjamin Constant across the Amazon —Solimoes now in Brazil—from Tabatinga. Waiting. Waiting for a big boat to take them to Manaus. Some say it will come this afternoon; others, tomorrow or the next day. At noon the tables fill up, then are deserted once more in the long afternoon of tropical heat. The two students practice Portuguese. Laura writes in her journal.

David tiptoeing in the door, holding a ragged bouquet of wildflowers and a bottle of wine. Laura turns her head away.

"A friend of mine has land in the Sangre de Cristo mountains," David says. "Let's go for a long weekend."

"Is this an apology?"

"The best I can do," David says, proffering the limp flowers, head cocked to one side.

The corners of her lips twitch, then the smile pours out.

"There's bears in them thar mountains," he threatens, tackling her onto the couch. Laura giggles, then flips him onto the floor.

"How did you do that?"

But Laura is running out the door, laughing.

Laura and the students, three days later, board the Itapuranga, bound for Manaus. A big boat, whose loud engine propels it night and day along the vast Solimoes.

At night on the upper deck, the bright stars seem close at hand. The wind is fresh off the water, the jungle a dark background. Laura sees the occasional light of a small boat in the black vastness.

The next morning the sky is streaked, alternating dark cloud and yellow, and the jungle emerges into greater clarity. Smoke rises from the cooking fire of a lone hut.

Laura has risen early and sits alone on the upper deck, gazing across the water.

A sudden quarrel of parrots in the tree tops at the water's edge. A gibbous moon paling in a pearl sky.

"May I sit down?" asks a small compact man. Then, "Would you like a beer?"

"Certainly," Laura answers to the first question, but declines the beer.

The dark-haired man is a doctor.

"What do you specialize in?"

"Gynecological oncology."

"Oh, but how depressing that must be."

"I get all kinds of cases, some brought in from the jungle. Quite fascinating."

His thick mobile eyebrows rise in the center, and the corners of his mouth curve upward, giving him a puckish look.

"I'm also a Congressman."

He opens his wallet and shows Laura a picture of himself with the daughter of the President, then another of himself giving a speech in Parliament.

"It's quite dangerous here. Politicians all have bodyguards—they fear for their lives. A Wild West atmosphere," he says cheerfully, taking another sip of beer. "Are you sure you won't have one?"

"No, no," Laura says, "It's six in the morning."

He opens another beer.

"You know what they say: Brazil is a melting pot of three races—the native Indians, imported African slaves, and Portuguese gangsters." He laughs to himself. "You wouldn't believe what it's like."

Sydney and Jacob, the two graduate students, arrive on deck. They are learning Portuguese and soon are deep in conversation with the doctor, who has abandoned his halting English. Laura slips quietly away. She leans against the rail, gazing at the vast Solimoes.

But she sees the whitecaps on Lake Palestine. Soft laughter and the clink of ice in a Scotch and soda. Clayton is standing next to the brunette, the brown of her slim legs startling next to the white shorts, and Laura can see it happening. Clayton is a successful dermatologist now, trim and boyish in yacht clothes. The brunette has just graduated from Brown, with the perfect confidence of the young, for whom the world opens wide, beckoning.

In the afternoon the Itapuranga docks at Santo Antonio do Ica, a town cradled in the curve of the Ica River where it flows into the Solimoes. A band amplified by giant speakers plays the vibrant, driving north Brazilian music on the narrow waterfront plaza below the bluff, where a crowd has gathered. Girls sway to the music, boys leap off the dock, and small children climb up on roofs above the band. Canoes paddle out into the harbor. Boys clamber onto the Itapuranga and leap from the upper deck into the river. The boat to Manaus has arrived!

Laura leans over the rail to watch dock workers shining with sweat lift big cases of empty liter beer bottles from stacks on the dock. A large black man tosses a case to a compact brown one, who in the same motion swings it down into the hold: toss, catch, toss, in a steady rhythm. Other hands load big stalks of bananas. The locals canoe in lumber, great heavy boards, twelve feet long, ten inches thick, heart wood so heavy it takes four men to lift each plank.

Now the sun has gone down, and the water darkens. Laura watches the last buzzard flying home for the night above the vast silent jungle. The boat sounds its horn, and the boys come out of the water.

The boat pulls away and leaves behind the crowd overflowing the narrow plaza. A few boys jump back in the water while the band plays on, growing fainter in the distance.

The town's few lights glimmer, and its palms are dark against the tropical sky.

Now no lights are visible, and the shore is a dark line against the distant rose-tinted sky. Silence—undergirded by the rumble of the boat's massive engine.

Laura sips a beer on the upper deck. In the black night, two falling stars fade over the Amazon.

More stars than Laura has seen since she was a child, sitting on a fence rail with a friend while the horses, just unsaddled, blow out their breaths in the perfumed air of an East Texas summer night.

"You girls come in for supper now," her mother calls.

Laura blinks in the light, bright after the pine dark night outside. The girls sit quietly while Ola Mae serves rolls hot from the oven and the adults talk politics.

"Congressman Jakel comes close to being aptly named," a friend of the family says. Laura's father, owner of the small-town newspaper, laughs, but says nothing.

Laura examines the filigree of the heavy silver fork and waits for the moment when she can ask to be excused. Up in her room she and her friend will talk and giggle until lights out, then whisper in the dark.

The next morning a fine drizzle mists the Amazon. At intervals, a lone cabin with streaked boards and rusty tin roof huddles at the water's edge.

From an isolated hut in the jungle, a woman is standing at the window looking out into the grey stillness, and a man steps silently into the canoe moored nearby. The tin roof is shiny and new, the unpainted boards as yet unstained: seedpod of a life newly opened.

In front of the boat, two white herons fly above the water against a misty background; their wings flash bright, drawing light out of their colorless surroundings.

Now more and more houses appear along the bank. Then the boat chugs into the harbor of Manaus, jungle city on the Rio Negro just above its confluence with the Solimoes, once the opulent, roaring city of the rubber barons, battened on the blood of Indian slaves, accessible only by boat. Downtown, the great glittering domed opera house, Teatro Amazonas, built during the fantastic rubber boom.

Laura, the two graduate students, and Carl, a young Australian staying at the same hostel, walk out into the night from the opera house, with its chandeliers of Italian crystal and French bronze, its columns and balconies of English cast iron, its fantastic cupola made of tiles imported from France, its main curtain showing the goddess Iara presiding over the meeting of the waters, painted in Paris by a Brazilian artist. The music lingers with them.

Laura and Carl walk side by side a little ahead.

"How did you meet your girlfriend?" she asks.

"She's Canadian, and I was working in Montreal before I came here. In a month I'm going home to work in my father's business. I hope she'll like Australia. We've talked about it."

Clayton and I never talked, Laura thinks. He assumed I would fit my life to his. And I did.

Laura remembers the excitement of choosing a house and decorating it for the life Clayton provided. Fundraisers for the opera: regional stars in her living room singing to a select group sipping champagne—Vissi d'arte. Celeste Aida. Christmas parties when a north wind blew across the plains, and inside the conversation rose as the liquor flowed, and the firelight danced behind its glass screen.

So much work, for such a brief moment, yet suspended in time, lingering down the hallway of years.

Now in the Mirante Bar—a restaurant on a barge permanently docked to the Manaus wharf—the band plays loud. Laura sips her beer, waiting for the Moreira, her next boat, to finish loading.

Long summer days at girls' camp in the East Texas woods, hot smell of pine, strong young bodies illuminated by flickering firelight. Laura excels at woodcraft.

It is the last day, and all the parents are crowded around the ring. Laura's horse sidesteps as she rides into the center of the ring to accept the trophy. Laura's eyes are shining.

Brown and chigger-bitten and exhilarated, she goes home with a basketful of ribbons, mementoes, memories.

Then the end of childhood.

Laura sets her beer down abruptly. She walks past the throbbing band, music coursing through her blood, and climbs down the ladder to the dock. Mingling with the crowd gathered at one edge of the wharf, Laura stares at the vast expanse of the Rio Negro. A huge pink dolphin breaks the surface, droplets of water sliding down the sleek pink sides into the curl of the splash, as it vanishes into the depths.

Laura turns back. Near the Mirante Bar, stevedores are loading the hold of the Itapuranga for its return journey up the Solimoes. A young man unloads large bags of corn from a boxcar; in one smooth motion swings them out of the car onto his back, then slams them into a pile on the dock. A fine dust rising from the heavy bags of corn has settled on the smooth brown skin of his face, on his sturdy bare legs and feet. A blue cloth tied above his broad open face covers his hair. For a moment he stands erect, like a young Adonis, legs apart, in a yellow pile where a sack has broken and spilled. Golden corn covers his feet, rises about the strong sculpted calves. He returns Laura's smile with a smile of infinite sweetness.

In the still, cold air before the state Capitol, the voices of the carolers blend and swell. On impulse Laura has joined the group, with rousing renditions of Good King Wenceslaus and We Three Kings. Now, as the strains of O Holy Night linger in the air, Laura looks up to catch the eye of a man, fiftyish, whose sudden smile makes him look boyish.

"I know where we can get hot mulled wine," he says.

Laura surprises herself by following him to a quiet bar where they sit in a worn booth.

David is semi-retired, but as a software designer, he has never kept regular hours.

"Let's go to Africa," he says, and Laura thinks, Oh, wouldn't it be fun.

"The weekend probably wouldn't be long enough," she says drily.

David laughs, but before they leave, he has her phone number, and it's not long before they are taking weekend jaunts.

Not far from the Itapuranga, the Moreira is docked. A little smaller than the Itapuranga—and quainter, with carved wooden doors to the bathrooms, decoratively molded sinks—the Moreira will be Laura's home for the next four days as she and the graduate students travel south, southwest up the Rio Madeira.

Laura leans against the boat rail watching the endless procession on the Manaus wharf below while loud music booms from the upper deck. Vendors come aboard selling fruit, crackers, sweets, complete meals; calculators, sun glasses, candles, hammock ropes. A middle-aged woman helps an old woman aboard, while below young women and girls in skimpy tops and shorts stroll past. On the dock, a man balances a great box on his head, while another pulls a two-wheeled cart holding an even bigger box. Stevedores ride high on a truckload of oranges behind the line of family and friends waiting on the wharf. A young man lingers over a last kiss, then bolts aboard, leaving his girlfriend in the crowd.

The poignance of young love, Laura thinks. She remembers warm summer nights, slow dancing on the pavilion overlooking the lake, the sweet smell of the gardenia crushed against her shoulder.

Of all the young men, why Clayton? She has never asked herself that question before. Certainly he was suitable. Slim and good-looking, ambitious, good family. Why not Clayton? Yet how does one explain the current that draws two people together, youth that says: This one and no other, ever.

She turns away and looks toward the harbor. It is full of boats. On one, a giant crane many stories high is silhouetted against the orange and gold streaked sky. Behind Laura, the sky grows bluer behind the old customs house on the quay.

To the west, the sky now grows richer, and the immense silhouette of the crane starker. The sky darkens as the sun drops into the Rio Negro, and the crane is a black skeleton looming against the burnt orange and deep, deep red.

On the upper deck, to the beat of loud music, tables fill. Two tables over from Laura and the graduate students, Sydney and Jacob, an older couple sit side by side. A second man sips beer with them. The older woman's arms and shoulders flow with the music, one thin hand dangling a cigarette. Her eyes invite Laura to join in, and her face lights up when Laura begins to sway to the music. Sydney flushes with embarrassment. When the three stand up to leave, the couple nod to Laura. The other man crosses to her table, takes Laura's hand, then presses his heart with his other hand; he gives her one last lingering look as she leaves.

Now the Moreira is pulling away from Manaus to the poignant strains of a slow love song, passing the Mirante Bar and Restaurant, leaving behind the harbor lights under a clear black sky.

David holds her hand while the waves crash against the pier and clouds obscure the moon. She turns toward him as the clouds drift past the moon, and in the momentary illumination their eyes meet.

The true poignance of middle-aged love, the safe harbor after wild storms of youth. Deeper rooted, if less flamboyant passion.

Laura remembers Clayton, more and more ambitious, rarely home. Cancelled dinner plans, late nights of "work." Then the accusations, revelations, recriminations, and all the hurt.

Laura sits in the lawyer's office in a cool beige suit, erect in the leather upholstered armchair. Across the wide gleaming table the lawyer asks if she has any questions. She has not retained her own lawyer—it's a world she has never entered; Clayton has always handled all that. She shakes her head, wanting only to leave, to close a door behind her.

It is almost a year before she realizes what a fool she has been.

On the second deck, a profusion of hammocks of variegated colors hangs like a flock of narrow-winged, multi-colored butterflies frozen in flight. The hammocks fill every available space, so close together that Laura's hangs scarce a foot from the man on one side of her and would have been smack up against Jacob's (the other graduate student) except that she has strung hers higher than his.

Down the center of the boat, boxes and bundles, packs and bags are piled together. People packed densely in a small space: families with babies and small children, old women, single men. Yet one's hammock is a private place, a closed door.

Laura settles into her hammock, wrapped in the drone of the boat engine.

After the divorce, life on her own. No longer the big house, but an apartment. To her surprise, Laura finds technical writing fairly well paid, and the mastery of detail challenging. She remembers the thrill of putting down the first payment for her own modest house.

What would it have been like if she had had a child?

Christmas, and Clayton removes the little stocking hanging by the fireplace, tenderly. Laura lies on the couch, a tear trickling down her cheek, and Clayton brushes her hair with a kiss.

Yet he is quickly back into his routine, with little to say at home. Laura is sick for a long time.

It is morning now. On the upper deck, Laura sits in the shade of the bar and watches the jungle slip by. In a clearing, egrets cluster among Zebu cattle, white against the charcoal gray of a cow. Wild morning glories trail along the red riverbank above the muddy brown water of the Madeira.

A girl of eighteen dances to loud music in shorts and halter top under the fierce tropical sun. She sweeps past Laura's table with two young men, her face flushed and her skin already reddening in the merciless sun. She laughs aloud, her body moving sinuously to the beat of the music.

In the evening she comes to Laura, holding her hot, swollen breasts.

"They hurt. I left my baby."

Laura rubs aloe vera lotion on the child's sunburned back and shoulder.

"She's one. I left her with my brother."

Separated from her husband, or impulsively leaving him to follow her great love to Porto Vehlo. Laura understands just enough Portuguese to catch the drift.

"I must have been crazy."

"But I'll never go back," she adds after a moment.

"I have no money, not one real. I would be much obliged if you could help me."

Laura rubs more lotion into the hot reddened skin and pretends she doesn't understand.

The girl thanks her, then drifts to the group of old women sitting on a bench along the side of the boat. One wrinkled old woman listens earnestly, then takes the girl's hand and gives her a warm smile.

At Humaita, the Moreira pulls to the shore for a brief stop. A few passengers disembark to buy sandwiches from vendors on the muddy riverfront. Sydney stands near Laura on the boat. They watch as the girl walks the long steep steps up the river bank. Sydney, whose Portuguese is much better, says that the girl had a fight with her boyfriend just as they were leaving Manaus, and he didn't get on the Moreira with her. As Laura gazes upward, she sees the girl enter a taxi with a man. The highway is good to Porto Velho, the trip a matter of hours rather than the full day by boat. The car door slams and the girl disappears toward Porto Velho and her fate.

The Moreira resumes her hypnotic journey up the mud-colored Madeira. Jungle lives pass by as in a dream. Two horses, a bay and a dun, graze in a cleared strip. Two canoes are moored nearby. More jungle, then a cluster of buildings—two houses, a barn, a chapel. Kingfishers and herons fly before the boat. A swarm of butterflies, yellow and orange, then a single green one. Brahma cattle graze in a narrow cleared strip near a wooden loading chute that opens directly onto the water. Unbroken undergrowth. A sow with a swarm of piglets dashes around a bare mud yard shaded by big trees, and a white chicken runs down the red bank.

So many years slipping by. Drinks after work with friends, the occasional movie.

Laura is propped up in bed reading, the TV muted, the cat curled at her feet. The lamp makes a pool of light on the old fashioned double bed that was hers as a child—her grandmother's bed. She has put a lot of thought into making her small house comfortable, even elegant in its simplicity. She will turn out the lights soon. In the morning she will pick up coffee and a croissant on the way to work.

Life growing narrower and narrower—until David blows it open.

David's rumpled hair in the morning next to her. He gets up first and starts the coffee while she clings to the last wisps of sleep.

"There's a moonlight hike tonight at Wild Basin," he says, looking at the paper as she enters the kitchen. A couple of dead leaves have fallen on the floor from the morning paper, but David hasn't noticed. The early light falls across his strong, capable hands, surprisingly well kept.

"Let's bike to the Rainbow for breakfast," he says. "It won't be crowded this early."

And now Laura is wide awake, biking down a shady street with a cool breeze lifting her hair.

So often David surprises her with long weekend getaways: hiking familiar pine forests, biking up wild mountain paths, racing along coastal sands.

Then the trip to Africa.

"You really mean it?"

"I said so the night we met."

And there it is: the red sun enormous as it casts its last rays across the dusty yellow grass. Laura clutches her camera, but she carried pictures in her mind: long necked giraffes with their innocent, above-it-all gaze, shambling elephants.

Later, the sounds of an African night as they lie in a tent after a long day in the Land Rover bumping across the veldt in search of lions.

Deep well of passion so different from the bright rippling brooks of youth. And a comfortable acceptance of life a little worn around the edges.

Now at Porto Velho, Laura and the graduate students leave the Moreira to travel by bus to Rio Branco, then Sena Madureira, a town of mud streets where the Iaco and the Purus Rivers meet. They have entered a world where there are no other gringos.

From the small boat, Laura scanned the jungle undergrowth. The Purus was an intimate river, unlike the great Solimoes, unlike the large Madeira. An old man walking along the bank hurried to the water's edge. A small man, he carried a shotgun across one shoulder and in the other hand a bucket holding a hindquarter of venison, one hoof sticking out of the bucket. He spoke to the captain, then climbed aboard.

The old man walked past Laura to the rear of the boat. Their eyes met and he smiled.

"Hi," Laura said, exhausting her Portuguese.

His face lit up.

"Good morning," he said.

Mid-morning the boat pulled into the bank.

"Do you want to walk a little way?" Jacob, the graduate student, asked Laura. "The Purus turns and twists so sharply in S-turns that in places you can walk across much faster than the boat can travel."

The captain, a few crew members, the old man, and Laura and the graduate students slipped into the jungle. They passed banana palms, with bunches of green bananas hanging high above their heads.

The path climbed steeply and came to a fence. In the rear, Laura wondered why it was taking so long for everyone to crawl through the cross bars, but when it was her turn, she saw a big snake, red and gray, lying across the trail on the other side. She started, then saw it was dead. The old man waited for her.

"What is it called?" the old man asked in Spanish.

"Snake," Laura said.

"Esnake," the old man repeated, and then the two walked on together.

The path led to a cluster of huts high on the riverbank. Pigs, sheep, chickens, three dogs and a cat shared the hard-packed dirt. Brahma cows wandered nearby. Some of the small children had very large distended bellies. From a hammock a child cried continuously, its arms and legs like sticks. The mother tried to give it liquid from a spoon, then sponged the child off with water, the child feebly crying and crying and crying. Finally the mother, holding the youngest baby, crawled into the hammock until the older child's cries eventually subsided.

Laura sat on a log before the remains of a fire near the old man while the boatmen bartered with the natives, a pig for a bag of salt. Pigs and piglets and chickens busily scavenged, while a couple of skinny dogs, ribs and hipbones showing, gently played just a moment, then lay in the dirt. On the porch of a nearby hut, a squirrel monkey scampered out of sight.

Orange, tangerine, and grapefruit trees loaded with fruit dotted the clearing. The men filled bags full to take back to the boat.

"No one eats the grapefruit," the captain said, "just the pigs."

But Laura and the graduate students gathered a few along with the tangerines and oranges.

One of the crewmen gave Laura his hand as she slid down the muddy bank. And while she ate tangerine after tangerine, dropping the peels into the dark water, two of the men continued shaking down tangerines and tossing them to crew members on board. Laura and the graduate students split two big grapefruit, still warm from the tropical sun. The sun splintered onto the boat, filtered through the foliage.

Suddenly Laura wanted her hammock. She wrapped sadness and the hammock around her. At the close of day, she still lay crumpled in her hammock.

To talk to David. Or simply to walk together along the seashore, while the gulls cry overhead. Or to be companionably ensconced in separate books, sprawling on the big bed. Or to slice and dice together in the kitchen, celebrating the wine gods with friends.

To come alive in late middle age, the petals of the soul slowly opening, expanding in a full blossoming.

To behold death. "David," she cried as he staggered, face contorted. "David," the long wailing cry as he dropped.

Stone dead before he hit the floor, the doctor said.

After nightfall, the old man walked to the back of the boat past her hammock, a comforting presence. She nodded to him in the darkness.

One by one, the crew, the graduate students, the old man, crawled into their hammocks. Laura carefully arranged the folds of her mosquitero, slapped at the handful of mosquitoes that had entered with her. She hugged herself in the dark and sobbed silently.

The next morning before first light, the men emerged from their hammocks, splashed themselves with muddy river water. Laura walked across the damp sand over a small rise in the graying light. She flinched when she saw a figure appear at a distance, but it turned out to be Sydney. They walked back across the sand together to the boat. As Laura stood washing the mud and sand from her feet, the captain offered them a glass of milky coffee. She sipped the hot sweet liquid gratefully as the boat started up.

The rising sun, though itself invisible behind jungle and cloud, touched some of the grey clouds above the tree line with rose. Under the overcast sky, the air was cool.

The boat pulled up near the muddy river bank long enough for a crewman to cast a net into the water. The first throw brought up half a dozen mantega, small edible fish; subsequent throws, nothing.

The sun was high now and the sky blue with a few white cumulus, the air warmer.

A big butterfly with black and light blue wings floated by. At the river's edge, Laura saw a russet-backed oropendula, a bird that has a nest like a falling teardrop. The day before, walking in the jungle, Laura had seen a moth as big as a bird.

Laura sat cross-legged on the plastic tarp covering the bags of salt and sugar. The warm air enveloped her and the steady drone of the motor lulled her. She meditated, drawing in the light. The old man walked by and Laura's eyes fluttered open. He reached out his hand and touched the top of her head with a wondering, delighted look.

Laura caught the word "sun."

"Don't stop," he said. And Laura drifted back into the light.

The next day they reached the confluence of the Chandless and the Purus. The old man gathered up the shotgun he had made the long journey downriver to have repaired, and a small sack. His two sons waited at the dock with a canoe. As they paddled off up the Chandless, Laura put her hand to her heart. She wanted to stop him, wanted to paddle with him up the narrowing Chandless, into the dark encompassing jungle.

She turned back to the boat and it seemed empty.

At dark the boat moored at a sandy beach under a three-quarter moon. For the first time, the mosquitoes were unbearably fierce. The graduate students left the boat and set up their tent on the beach in the moonlight. Laura retreated into her hammock under the mosquitero with a flashlight and book. She read a little, then turned off the flashlight and lay still. Some of the boatmen had no mosquiteros and Laura listened to the steady slap, slap, of hands against mosquitoes. One of the men played a cassette, a melodic love song. Easy laughter punctuated the low murmur of voices. Moonlight flooded the beach.

How strange to be on this small boat—on a muddy river in a native reserve under a Brazilian sky, far away in miles, and even more in time, from her own accustomed life. Yet Laura felt comfortable, at home.

Home is the evanescence of a journey. It is floating down a river where a cayman slides into the water before you and a heron cranks in the air above, she thought.

Laura awoke from a doze and slipped from her hammock into the moonlight. The gibbous moon hung low in the west, the dark silhouette of the forest reflected again in the darker waters of the Purus. The moonlight lay like a spell on the boat. Everyone slept but Laura. The frogs were hushed, the slow suspiration of the jungle silent.

Days, weeks, a lifetime, careening through love and loss, mistake and creation—all leading to this moment: a Brazilian moon hung low over the tree tops, its reflection rippling across dark waters to plunge straight into the crown of Laura's head where the journey of soul and self merged in an illumined night under a sky of silent stars.

Laura returned to her hammock. She saw the moon drop lower and the haze move in to blur it. The silent boat moored in the dark river seemed to rock her hammock, rock her until she fell into a deep and dreamless sleep.

Texas Portraits

Epitaph for a Cow

"Hyah, hyah!"

"Keep 'er going, keep 'er going. Don't let 'er stop."

The cow slammed into the fence, half turned, and lowered her head. Joey ran at her, waving his arms and hollering, not giving her a chance to think. He stampeded her down the chute through the only opening—the back of the trailer. I shoved the steel gate down the track, ran around to the other side and dropped the heavy steel pins into the slots. I had to hammer and twist the top one to force it down.

"Ever hear of WD40?" Joey was grinning.

He climbed up one side of the weathered wooden chute, carefully avoiding the rotten board. He swung over lightly, holding onto the steel rail at the top of the trailer.

Which set off the cow again. A growth blocking one eye, she was literally half blind, able to see everything to the left, but nothing on her right.

Slinging slobber, she tried to turn around, skidded in fresh, wet manure to her knees, then recovered.

"Better keep moving," I said, starting the pick-up.

A few hazy clouds drifted in the sky, softening the sunlight reflected off the highway.

The vet came out to the trailer, studied the cow for a long time. He shifted the wad in his cheek.

"It's cancer," he said. "See that white tumor in the eye? That's just the tip of it. Nothing I can do. Sell her. You won't get much, but usually some buyer will gamble that enough of the carcass'll pass inspection."

"Okay," I said.

Hey, I don't make the laws, I just follow them.

"Carl says he never saw a cancer in the early days, but here lately three or four of his cows have showed up with it," I remarked.

"The only ones I see it in drink from the river," the vet said. "I see a lot, now that Williamsville discharges its treated sewage into the San Sebastian."

"Yeah, and Graylor pumps its municipal water from that river, downstream from Williamsville," I said.

And if you're one of those citizens, that's your lookout. Me, I drink well water.

"Call Bobby Lee. He'll probably take her today," the vet said, looking back at the cow.

"Yeah, we'd never get her back in the trailer. Half blind like that, she was acting crazy."

Nobody answered at the auction barn. The auction is Wednesday and receives Tuesday, but this was only Monday.

"Wellington's auction is tomorrow," a hefty man in the vet's waiting room said.

"They'll be taking 'em today," said the leathery man sitting next to him. Wellington is a pretty good drive, but heck, Carl pays us by the hour.

Outside, Joey was leaning against a dark blue pick-up, talking to Esther Dubacek. He never misses a chance.

"C'mon. We're going to Wellington."

As I drove into Graylor, the cow became more and more agitated. By the time I reached the third light, the left side of the town that the cow could see had panicked her. She *was* a country cow. Sometimes, in the metropolis to the southwest, I felt that way myself.

As I started down a steep incline heading east out of town, the cow worked herself into a frenzy. She had retreated to the back end of the trailer and now was slamming back and forth against the sides.

"Damn," Joey said, looking back.

The trailer whipped back and forth, the cow stomping and bellering and crashing into the sides. I gripped the steering wheel hard, trying to hold it steady. My foot was off the accelerator, but I couldn't brake without jack-knifing the pick-up.

Down the steep incline the truck picked up speed, faster and faster. My knuckles white against the steering wheel, I felt like I was wrestling an alligator.

"Goddamn," Joey said.

The trailer jerked the pick-up rhythmically as it whipped from side to side in ever greater undulations.

Traffic behind and before hastily pulled off to the side of the road.

As we raced down the incline toward the overpass at the bottom, the trailer snapped back and forth in larger and larger arcs. I clung hard to that bucking bronco.

Joey said nothing.

Suddenly the trailer reached its limit and flipped on its side, the heavy metal tongue twisted by the torque of the trailer. The drag from the heavy steel trailer slowed the pick-up, and I gently lined it up against the curbing on the side of the road.

Joey and I looked at each other.

I took a deep breath and stepped out of the truck.

"Look at that," Joey said.

The cow had scrambled out of the overturned trailer, crossed the asphalt, and climbed the embankment on the other side of the highway. Now she was dancing across the graves in the city cemetery.

I started up the steep embankment on the right side of the road. When I reached the weathered house at the top, an old woman met me at the door.

"C'mon in. Done called the police. Saw it out my window."

The pungent smell of collard greens filled the small kitchen. A pot steamed on the stove next to the sink, which looked out over the highway below.

I called Carl. When I looked back out the window, a cop car with its flashing lights stood next to the pick-up and a policeman was talking to Joey.

The cop looked up as I stumbled down the bank. His ticket pad was open, a perplexed look on his face. For the first time I noticed the deep rut the trailer had gouged the length of the asphalt some thirty yards.

"Now, boys," he said.

"The cow went crazy, got a momentum going, and the trailer just flipped," I said.

"But . . ." the young officer began.

A weather-beaten rancher who had pulled over stepped heavily out of his pick-up.

"Son," he said gravely to the cop, "these things just happen sometimes."

The cop gave up, put his pad away, began to direct traffic. The trailer, sprawled like a flipped-over turtle, blocked half the highway.

Carl pulled up in his maroon, extended cab Dodge Ram and got out with a big jack. Amazed, I watched the heavy trailer slowly right itself as I pumped the jack handle.

"Carl, where'd you get this trailer, anyhow?"

"Had it built in 1955. Last time this happened was 'bout twenty years ago. Old man Heflen borrowed it to haul some cows. Got to going too fast and when it started whipping, he hit the brakes."

By this time I had the trailer upright.

"Just park it over there off that gravel road."

I unhitched the trailer from my old gray Chevy and followed Carl, who wheeled his big pick-up around, crossed the highway, and took the drive up the hill into the cemetery. Way at the far corner the cow grazed quietly next to a crooked headstone. Joey leaned on one hip smoking a cigarette.

"Bobby Lee'll be here any minute," Carl said. "He said next time for you boys just to put anything you got in the pens, let him know later."

I walked over to a bush, relieved myself.

When I stepped back, Carl clapped me on the shoulder. "You mean you held it in, Bill?"

Bobby Lee pulled up with his large, multi-sectioned livestock trailer. He climbed stiffly down from the truck cab.

He swung open the trailer gate, backed out a big chestnut gelding, already saddled. The cow jerked her head up, moved farther away.

Grunting, Bobby Lee hauled himself up into the saddle, shook out his lariat. The huge horse stood placidly.

They moved out, the great rounded hindquarters of the horse working smoothly. Joey leaned toward me. "Look at the rear on that horse. You could rope a freight train offa him."

The cow looked up, sidled off. Bobby Lee put his heels into the chestnut, and the big horse lumbered into action. Tail high, the cow took off, the huge horse in a rocking canter after her.

The cow scrambled across a grave, one foot sinking in the soft loam, then raced across three others. The chestnut pulled close, and Bobby Lee made a try. He missed, and the loop fell harmlessly to the ground. Bobby Lee muttered under his breath.

The cow grew canny. She dodged behind a gravestone and made a twisting run toward the center of the cemetery, the big gelding right behind her.

"Good thing there ain't no services today," Joey said.

Bobby Lee kicked the big chestnut into high gear, and the gelding cut the cow off. She wheeled, trampled a couple more graves, then cut to the left. The chestnut stomped over the same graves and turned almost instantaneously with the cow. She doubled back, the gelding matching her move for move, and they galloped across a neighboring row of graves.

On her blind side, the cow stomped a bouquet of flowers, scattering artificial rose petals in her wake. The big gelding strode through a light dusting of plastic petals, his eyes fixed on the cow. She leapt the curbing of a stately collection of graves and cut behind a granite obelisk erected in memory of the McDermott family.

The big chestnut followed her into the aisle between graves and caught up on her blind side in the middle of a wide grave near a tilting headstone.

Bobby Lee swung, and the loop settled gracefully around the cow's neck. The gelding braced himself. The cow hit the end of the rope, slammed into the ground, and ploughed up another grave scrambling to her feet. Bobby Lee hauled her to the trailer, the big gelding keeping the rope taut. I got behind her, and Joey slammed an inner gate shut when she reached the end of the trailer.

His job done, the huge gelding stood quietly, occasionally shifting his weight from one leg to the other.

Bobby Lee drove the big rig, with the gelding sectioned off from the cow in the back of the trailer, carefully down the narrow cemetery drive.

"Guess I'll get something for her at auction," Carl said. "Maybe enough to pay Bobby Lee."

Maybe you're thinking about that cow with cancer, how your kids eat at all these burger places. Well, Carl, Bobby Lee, they're just making a living—like the next guy. Just like the hamburger chains.

A dark blue pick-up turned in one arm of the cemetery drive as Carl was driving off down the other. Joey's eyes lit up. Even when he was in high school he liked his women a little older. I have to admit, Esther Dubacek is a good-looking woman. Strong, too. I resigned myself to a little wait.

She stopped not far off, and Joey was nearly to the cab when she got out. She held a bouquet of flowers.

"Hi, again," Joey said.

"What are you doing here?"

"Oh, just a little business."

"In the *cemetery*? You're not mixed up in something you shouldn't be?"

"No, no. What'er you doing here?"

"It's my aunt's anniversary. Funny, I passed Bobby Lee just now. I wonder . . ."

Esther stopped stock-still, staring at her aunt's grave. A wet pile gleamed moistly in the sunlight. She looked at Joey.

"Carl's cow got loose. That's why Bobby Lee. . . . I'm sorry about your aunt. Wasn't no disrespect—just a accident." Joey composed his face and put a soothing tone in his voice.

I stepped around to the other side of my old gray pick-up, looked up at a few clouds drifting high overhead. Wished I had a Coke.

When I walked back around, Esther was saying, "I need a man who's strong, but knows how to be gentle with a woman."

"That's me," Joey said, giving her a long lingering look.

"I need a hard worker, but a man who likes to have a good time."

"That's me," Joey said, strutting a little, his chest puffed out.

"I need a man who can be a good father to my three kids."

"That ain't me," Joey said, looking quickly around. He caught my eye.

"C'mon," I called over. "We got fences to fix."

Handler Road

"Hell, Billy Bruce ain't no problem."

"Then how come them 'dozers setting out there at the end of Handler Road?" I asked. "Edgar Thrum run them surveying boys off his place, but it didn't do no good."

I pulled the pickup in beside one of the big utility rigs.

"Aw, you just need a cup of coffee," Joey said, flashing that grin of his as we walked into the Oatville Store.

"Morning," I said to the utility crew drinking coffee at the big table in the front corner. The newly hired kid was sitting near the end, sprawled face down on the table.

"Wish I'd had that good a time last night," Joey said.

Joey poured two cups of coffee in the thick dark mugs and passed me one. He stirred three spoonfuls of sugar in his while looking all around. But there weren't any women this time of day, just June reading the paper at the back table.

"The county attorney says there's no conflict of interest in Commissioner Billy Bruce voting to extend Handler Road even though he owns all those shares in Metropolitan Water," June said, looking up from her paper.

"Hell, no. It's *in* his interest," I said. "Ain't no conflict about it."

The men at June's table laughed.

"He never would have passed English if June hadn't helped him," one said.

"That's because she was sweet on his brother."

"Wish I'd let him fail."

"Math must have been his strong suit."

"I don't know, the way he can make two plus two equal five—or fifty thousand."

"Fifty thousand is peanuts if they buy up enough of the Corvales Aquifer to fund all that development."

"This blackland's going to be covered in concrete. He's trying to get the County to build Handler Road so it can pay for the right of way for his waterline," June said.

"Dryerson County's real tough on crime—as long as it's the little fellow."

"That engineer that worked on the dam—the one building a house near the lake—he said Dryerson County was the most corrupt place he'd ever lived. And he's been all over," June said. "Said the inspectors kept coming back, wouldn't pass his septic tank 'till he paid them off."

"Don't steal a can of hairspray, though," I said.

"Or get caught with drugs," a younger man said.

Joey was fidgeting behind me.

"Come on," he said. "We got to get to work."

He never could stay still for long.

"You boys 'bout through fencing the Ahern place?"

"Naw, couple more days' work," I said.

"Be a week if you don't get going," Joey said. He headed for the door.

Already the early morning coolness was gone, and the rising sun promised another scorcher. The county road on the way to the Ahern place wound alongside the river, not far from the cliff's edge.

"That's where that carload of Mexicans went over, years ago," I said. "Before the dam was built."

"Good fishing down there," Joey said. "I've caught a few myself."

"Yeah, but I wouldn't eat 'em,"

"You worry too much. Look at it this way: something's going to get you, one way or the other. You might as well enjoy life while you got it."

"Like those Mexicans, too drunk to make the curve?"

"At least they died happy," Joey said, flashing that grin as he climbed out to open the gate into the Ahern place.

By ten our shirts were soaked, and the sweat was stinging my eyes.

"I'm ready for a Coke," I said, heading for the cooler. Joey kept on with the rhythmic clanging of the steel post driver until his post was driven in level with the line of posts we had sunk that morning.

A hawk circled lazily in the cloudless sky above as I dropped my bulk onto the grass in the shade of the pickup. Joey popped a Coke can and sprawled nearby.

"I feel sorry for them city boys," he said, gazing across the open pasture toward the pecan bottom. A crow cawed in the distance.

"Them city boys are fixin' to take it over if Billy Bruce gets his way."

"Come on," Joey said, tossing his empty can in the back of the pickup and grabbing the steel sleeve. Joey wasn't all that big, but he was wiry, and the truth was he could outwork me—and he knew it. I've seen bigger men attack those steel posts and huff and puff, but Joey had a rhythm, like he was on a dance floor, and those posts just seemed to sink into the ground.

By the end of the day, the posts were all in, and all that was left was to string the wire. We'd been through two gallons of water and a six pack of Cokes, and even Joey looked wrung out. He perked up, though, with a cold beer in his hand, sitting around a table at the Oatville Store. Only after a hard day's work was Joey willing to sit around.

"Hey," Joey said, grinning at Jolene.

"Hey yourself," she said as she passed by carrying a round of beer for the utility crew at the long table.

"Let me have some," Joey said, holding up his empty bottle but giving Jolene a meaningful look.

"Get your own," she said with a flounce of her blonde hair. But she pulled a cold Bud from the cooler and set it down in front of him.

Joey's eyes were bright, and there was a sparkle in hers, but the store was crowded and Jolene kept moving.

I looked at Joey.

"Aw, you worry too much. He's a trucker, gone for days—nights—at a time." Joey winked.

"Yeah, but if he ever finds out. . . ."

"Aw, he's all belly."

"A trucker's got some arms on him. And he's got the weight behind him."

"Don't lose any sleep," Joey said.

The next morning when I picked Joey up, he sauntered across the gravel to the truck, hopped in and yawned.

"Didn't sleep much, huh?"

Joey just grinned and winked.

In the Oatville Store, he grabbed a couple of big Styrofoam cups and said, "Come on, let's take it to go."

Today we were stringing the wire. Not as hard as driving posts, but you really have to pay attention to what you're doing. You want the wire tight, but if you over tighten it, that barbed wire can snap and do some real damage. Joey always liked this part. The corner posts were heavy wooden posts that were cross-braced, and the wire was stapled to them. But the barbed wire was fastened to the steel posts with short pieces of smooth wire.

Always a hard worker, Joey seemed to be speeding up the pace today.

"What's your rush?"

Joey had cut a handful of short lengths of smooth wire, and his hands seemed to be flying as he twisted each one tight around the barbed wire against the steel post with the wire tool. He had finished his post and moved on to the next one while I was still working on mine.

"I might take me a little longer lunch break."

"That trucker coming in tonight?"

"Yeah, but what he don't know won't hurt him. Plenty to go around."

"Meet you at the store around 2:00," Joey said when I dropped him off at the end of the gravel road leading to Jolene's. You could see the small frame house at the top of the rise back from the county road. A couple of big hackberries shaded the front yard. A creek behind the rise filled a tank, then flowed down to the county road, through a culvert, and eventually into the San Sebastian River. He grinned and headed up the drive.

The noon crowd filled the store—a couple of veterinarians, guys from the auction barn, a retired judge with his Mexican hands. I joined one of the vets. At his table were his receptionist and two assistants, all women, not bad looking.

"Where's Joey?"

"He had a little business to take care of. How close would Handler Road come to your new clinic?"

June set the plate of brisket, beans, and potato salad in front of me.

"Real close. Billy Bruce's wife owns land just south of there. I reckon he plans on developing it."

"Just that many more cats and dogs to take care of," the receptionist said.

"Ain't worth it."

"What about that place you lease?"

"The old Streatham place? Billy Bruce owns part of that too. Bought out one of the sisters, and the other's not too happy. Course she's got to keep quiet about it 'cause she has to have an easement to get to her half."

I emptied my Coke.

"Give me a Bud," I said when June passed by.

"Well, some of us have got to go to work." The veterinarian stood up and reached for his check. His fingers, though long, were so thick they looked stubby, and the piece of paper seemed awkward in his massive hands. The three women followed him out.

At 2:15 there was still no sign of Joey. I held up my empty bottle and June brought me another beer.

At 2:30 the door opened and Joey walked in with Joe Don, June's cousin. He was wet and muddy and had a scratch over one eye.

"Lemme have a Bud and a sausage wrap," he said to June, but Joe Don was already walking back from the cooler with two beers.

Joey gave me a wicked grin.

"Hitched me a ride with Joe Don."

"You never know what you're gonna find by the side of the road. I liked to get run over by one of them eighteen wheelers, slamming on the brakes when I saw old Joey coming up outta that bar ditch. Wet and muddy. Covered with beggar's lice. Looked like a old ditch rat."

Joe Don started laughing and a few people looked curiously over at our table.

The door opened and in walked Jolene's husband, George, staring wildly around.

"What can I do for you?" June asked quickly.

"Where is he?"

Conversation stopped and the store was suddenly quiet. Joey took a bite of his sausage wrap and Joe Don looked like he was enjoying his beer.

George glared all around, then walked up to our table.

"How'd you get so wet and muddy?"

"Rough job . . . if it's any of your business."

"I'm making it my business."

"Now hold on," I said. "You got no call to come interrupting our lunch."

"You stay out of this."

"Stay out of what? We're having lunch, minding our own business."

Joey finished off his sausage wrap, took a long sip of beer and stared noncommittally at George.

"I want to know how he got like that."

"He told you. We're fencing the Ahern place. It's a rough job, specially near that old slough."

"Well, he'd better stay . . ."

Joey pried a piece of gristle from between his teeth with a fingernail.

Joe Don remembered to take a swig of beer.

George looked baffled.

Joey looked at the clock on the far wall.

I took a sip of beer.

"If I catch you . . ."

"James, get two bags of range cubes, 20%, for Adolf," June called out.

The door opened and Hannah, a weathered, middle-aged woman who had a farm to the east, north of the river, walked up to the counter.

"How can I help you?"

Hannah bought a lottery ticket and looked around. She saw a woman she knew at the table next to ours and walked over.

"Excuse me," she said as she passed George and sat down next to her friend.

George looked from Joey to me, then turned abruptly and stormed out the door. Good thing Joe Don's back was to him. His mouth was twitching and it was all he could do not to let out a guffaw. Not Joey, though. He just drained the last of his beer and said, "We better get back to work."

"I could use me some Mexican food," Joey said, wiping the sweat off his face. We had worked until we finished the fence, and I was fagged out.

"Sounds good to me."

The sun was low in the west, and the fierceness of the day was past as I drove down the county road, past the curve where the Mexicans had gone off the bluff, and on into town.

It was cool and dim in Rosalita's.

"Lemme have a Bud."

"Make that two. And an order of nachos," I said. "Tommy Lee. What's going on?"

"Bill, Joey. Not much. How about you?"

"I hear the County has got a crew starting on Handler Road. What's this about the city passing a resolution supporting a county road?"

"Oh, you can't stand in the way of progress."

"You mean somebody's deep pockets. I hear Charlie Myers leaned pretty hard on the rest of you. Pretty convenient his employees signing that petition to support the road."

"Oh, you're likely to hear all kinds of things. But after all, you know the growth is coming this way. We've got to be foresighted and prepare for it."

"Prepare for it? By building a six-lane county road to nowhere, through 100-year-old family farms? Or drag it here?"

"Excuse me, fellows." Joey headed for the bar, winked at Angie.

"Now, Bill, you might just as well get used to it."

Angie set a Bud in front of me, a Miller Lite in front of Tommy Lee.

"Why?"

"It's gonna happen. Now what's this I hear about George storming in to the Oatville Store?"

"Oh, you know George."

"Yeah, and I know Joey."

"What do you know," Joey said, coming back to the table and straddling a chair turned backwards.

Tommy Lee motioned to Angie for another round. The door opened and several people entered.

"I know George and Jolene just walked in."

"Yeah," Joey said, not turning around, "everybody likes Rosalita's."

He smiled at Angie when she set the beers down, and she smiled back.

"Damn, Joey," Tommy Lee said, shaking his head. Then, "I guess I better go say hi."

The couple with George and Jolene live in town, and Tommy Lee never misses a chance to do a little politicking. I wouldn't say being a city councilman has gone to his head, but he probably surprised even himself when he got elected. His problems with alcohol and wives were notorious.

I signaled Angie for a couple more beers and she brought them along with our plates of enchiladas.

I have to say it about Joey, he may not be big, but he can sure put away the food.

When I stood up to go, Joey leaned back in his chair.

"I got me a ride home."

Angie passed by with a round of beer for George and Jolene's table and gave Joey a sidelong look. I just shook my head.

"See you in the morning."

A half moon had risen and the night air felt like a warm bath. When I stepped out of my pickup, in the deep silence the crunch of my boots on gravel sounded loud. I stood for a moment looking at the moonlight on the pasture. An owl hooted from the direction of the barn.

When my granddaddy bought the place, all he needed was enough money for the down payment, and the land paid itself off. And my daddy raised his family off the land. Not an easy life—we knew what hard work was—but a good life. My daddy didn't owe nobody nothing and he couldn't be fired. Hard to make a sheep out of a man like that. He believed what he believed, said what he thought, and couldn't nobody scare him.

My two dogs nuzzled me. Border collie, Australian shepherd crosses. Good cattle dogs.

I looked at the top of the ridge south of the house and imagined a line of houses on it, all the same, looking like a piece of the suburb plopped down. City folks made a mess out of their cities and they all want a piece of the country. But they don't even know what the country is.

"Okay, okay. I'll get you your supper."

The dogs were whining with eagerness as the dog food rattled into their dishes.

It's different today, what with the developers pushing up the price of land, the cost of big farm equipment so high while the price of crops goes down. No wonder some of them throw in the towel. Farmers the most productive they've ever been, but their sons can't buy land to make a living off, like in the old days.

The old pecan tree in the side yard cast a shadow in the moonlight, and the owl hooted softly again.

The red sun was just coming up when I picked up Joey, and a light mist seemed to rise from the pastures. It was just the right moment for the sun's rays to illuminate a row of orbweaver webs on the barbed wire fence.

"Lookit that," Joey said.

The intricate patterns shone silver in the pale light, each spider web anchored between two strands of barbed wire, and the several webs forming their own larger shimmering pattern. From a low branch of a hackberry sapling, another web shone, a long glimmering thread anchoring it to the dewy grass of the pasture.

When I pulled forward a few yards, the vision vanished. I backed up and the delicate, shining silver patterns reappeared.

"Ain't that something," Joey said in a hushed voice.

We were helping Carl Johnson work cattle this morning. The cattle were already in the catch pen when we drove up. Carl had a good set-up. Corrals made from used oil field pipes, good and solid. Didn't have to worry about a wild one tearing out the fence.

Carl had the wormer, the needles and blackleg vaccine, and the ear tags laid out on a table. His sixteen-year-old daughter, Nellie, stood nearby.

"Looking forward to school starting?" Joey asked.

Nellie made a face and Joey laughed.

"Wadn't my favorite thing, neither."

We soon got a rhythm going. Joey punched the cattle up, and as they crowded down the chute, I popped the lead one with the electric cattle prod so that it jumped into the squeeze chute. Carl pulled the lever just as the cow thought it was headed out, the steel bars catching it by the neck. Joey climbed up and painted the cow's back with the wormer, while I carefully slipped the needle through the tough hide into the hip and injected the blackleg vaccine. When we got to the calves, Carl clipped the tags into their left ears. Nellie kept the hypodermic needles filled with vaccine, and the tags inserted into the clipper.

"It's about time for a Coke," Carl said. The mid-morning sun burned hot in a cloudless sky, but the air in the corral above the milling herd of cattle looked hazy with the dust.

"That's my heifer," Nellie said, pointing to a big Charolais cross standing in the pen with other unworked cattle. Her tanned arm, flecked lightly with dust, glowed in the sunlight.

"Good looking," Joey said. "What are you going to do with her?"

"Breed her to that Branvieh bull we got. I can't wait to see what kind of calf I'll get."

"You heard anything more about Handler Road, Carl?" I asked.

"Naw, just that Billy Bruce downed him a six pack on the way to that meeting. But it don't matter how many of his neighbors oppose it, he's pushing that road through. They're all a bunch of crooks, if you ask me."

"It won't affect you much here, though."

"Not in the short term. But, hell, you know the country won't be the same after that bunch gets through crisscrossing it with roads. You take a guy like Billy Bruce. Flying to Colorado to a big deer lease, fancy lodge with the big boys. Goes to his head. It's a sickness we got in this country. Seems like a comfortable living ain't good enough any more. Everybody wanting more and more, and destroying the very thing that makes life worth living—this land."

"Seems like so many people can't see it any more, can't feel it," I said. "I guess if you grow up in one of them suburbs, don't never go outdoors except to get in your car, maybe something gets broke inside you."

"High school boys are so immature," Nellie said, giving Joey a sideways look.

"You just ain't found the right one yet," Joey said. "Be patient with them."

Carl stood up.

"We can get this knocked out in a couple more hours," he said.

By mid afternoon we were through. I had sweated through my cotton shirt, and a puff of breeze felt good against the wet cloth. Everyone was covered with dust, and even Nellie had a smear across her forehead where she'd wiped with a dusty hand.

"Want to see my mare? She's in the pasture behind the barn," Nellie said, stepping close to Joey.

"I'd like to, but we got to be going." Joey gave me a quick glance.

I grinned at Joey as I drove down the lane. "Scared of jailbait?"

"I ain't scared of nothing. But it ain't right. Give her another ten years and I'll be plenty interested."

"Let's go to the west end of the county, see what's going on. I hear they've already cut through Edgar Thrum's place."

"Naw, I got better things to do. Drop me off on Mesquite Street, 'bout the middle of the block between Third and Fourth."

I stopped in front of the small frame house Joey pointed out. Hollyhocks lined the sidewalk and potted plants covered the rail around the small porch. A gray cat observed the world from an old broken down arm chair.

"Meet you at Rosalita's for supper," Joey said. "Angie goes to work at five."

"We just ate there last night."

"I don't never get enough," Joey said, flashing that wicked grin as he started off up the walk.

Joey was sitting with a couple of guys from the County when I walked in Rosalita's. Several empty bottles stood on the table, but I was way ahead of those guys. Angie was already on her way over with a Bud when I sat down. Her face looked soft and she wore a private smile. Joey gave her a big open look as she set the beer down in front of me. She looked down and her smile grew more private as she returned to the bar.

The door opened and Tommy Lee walked in.

"Why, Bill, Joey, y'all hanging out here again?"

"I could say the same," I said, and motioned to Angie to bring me another beer. "The County done tore through Edgar Thrum's land. Where's it going to stop, Tommy Lee?"

"Depends. Just to County Road 1606 for now. But folks are going to want it all the way through."

"Yeah, and what did Edgar Thrum want? What do all the farmers around here want?"

"Well, I don't know. You know I represent the city."

Joey motioned Angie over.

"Let me have the beef enchilada plate. And a order of guacamole on the side."

"It comes with guacamole."

"Yeah, but I always want more," Joey said, looking straight at Angie.

She blushed and looked down at her pad, then turned toward the two County workers.

"Naw, we're leaving after this beer."

"Another Bud," I said.

"And to eat?"

"Hell, it don't matter. Give me the enchiladas."

Tommy Lee had drifted over to the next table.

"Where do you think you're . . ."

Joey grabbed me by the arm, hard.

"It ain't Tommy Lee. It's Billy Bruce you wanna hit."

"Yeah, well Billy Bruce ain't here."

"You want I should call and give him a invite?"

Joey started laughing, but I just glowered back.

He had made considerable progress through his enchiladas when Gene Kennedy stopped at our table.

"You boys starting that fence Monday?"

"Hell, no," Joey said. "Don't nobody work the first day of dove season."

"Where y'all going?"

"My cousin's got a lease down in South Texas. We'll start that fence Wednesday," I said.

Joey scraped his plate with a tortilla, then turned to what was left of the chips and hot sauce.

"Where do you put all that?" Gene asked, looking at Joey's wiry body.

"Why, it keeps me pore just packing all that food," Joey said, grinning as he stood to leave.

A light northerly breeze stirred the warm night air. I stood in my front yard a long time under the stars gazing at the south ridge, listening to the tree frogs and crickets. The dogs sat quietly, sensing my mood.

The bed creaked under my weight as I lay down. In the distance rose the wail and chatter of the coyotes as they swept down the fold between the ridges.

"You hear about Jason Scruggs?" June asked the Wednesday morning after we had gotten back from South Texas. I was pouring out our coffee.

"No."

"Tractor flipped over on him yesterday. He was mowing along the edge of the tank. Tractor pinned him under the water. When he didn't come in at suppertime, his wife sent the oldest boy out. Hard thing for him to find."

"How many kids did he have?"

"Four. The oldest is in high school, but the youngest is just in third grade. We've got a jar over there to take up a collection for the family."

Joey pulled a twenty out of his pocket and put it in the jar. I followed suit.

"Rosary is tomorrow," June said.

I knew I'd go, Joey too, if not to the rosary, to the funeral. But I'd be glad when it was over. I'm not much good when a woman's crying. Joey seems to know what to do, though. Me, I'd rather grub mesquite in August.

"How'd y'all do down in South Texas?" one of the regulars at June's table called out.

"Got our limit," Joey said. "Put 'em in Bill's freezer. One of these days we're gonna have a big blow out. Bill's got to get him one of them feral hogs first, though."

"Does it count if I run over one?"

"Flip your truck over," the guy at June's table said. "Night before last I was coming home, hit one on the county road and thought I was a goner. Right side of the truck lifted up and just as I thought I was going over, I hit one with the left tire. Just evened up and kept going."

Everybody laughed.

Joey drank the last of his coffee.

"Let's get going."

We pulled into the Kennedy place and headed for the back fence line. Rusted barbed wire sagged between wooden posts, some leaning at odd angles. The wire was brittle, broken and hanging in places, but firmly nailed into the old posts with heavy staples. Hackberry and bois d'arc saplings grew up at intervals along the fence. The ground was uneven, dipping down into hollows thick with dewberry vines.

Taking down an old fence is rough work, not clean and satisfying like building a new one.

"What a mess," I said. "Gene's really got it cut out for us."

"You don't know what fun is," Joey said, grabbing a chain saw out of the back of the pickup. "I'll start on the hackberries."

I pulled on a pair of work gloves and started wrenching staples out of the posts with a wire tool. Joey revved up the chain saw and attacked the saplings.

By the time the sun was high, we'd accomplished a lot, more than I thought we would.

"You know," Joey said, "letting a place go like this ain't all bad. No telling what's in them dewberry briars and them thickets. A well-taken-care-of place is pretty, but there's not so many foxes and rabbits and coons and such."

"And those sunflowers ought to bring the doves in. It's all a matter of balance."

"Yeah, take Jason Scruggs, now. He was a good man, but you ever notice how everything at his place always looked like it had a fresh coat of paint? Not a grass blade out of place. He was probably trying to get that last bit of grass on the side of the dam. Just pushed it too far. Nature's not like that. You got to live and let live."

"That oldest boy of his has the makings of a fine quarterback."

"Yeah, and he'll push that much harder, now," Joey said. "You never know. You're here one moment, gone the next. You just got to make the most of it while you got it."

I crumpled up the wrapper from my tuna fish sandwich and poured another glass of iced tea. The property on the other side of the fence line was heavily wooded with scrub elm and hackberry and an occasional tall pecan tree. Nearby, an arbor of grape vines hung from a stand of elms. A spring overflowed into a stream that meandered down the hillside into a small valley below.

Joey stepped over the rusty barbed wire now lying on the ground and walked down to the spring. He knelt on the rocky outcropping that formed a basin. Cupping the cool clear water in his hands, he splashed his face and neck.

"Boy, that feels good," he said, standing up and gazing off at the ridge where it curved south and west.

"If Billy Bruce has his way, that's where Handler Road will come through," I said, pointing toward the ridge.

"Come on," Joey said, pulling on heavy gloves and starting to roll up the old wire.

By 5:00, the fence line was cleared and the bed of the pickup piled high with coils of rusty wire and weathered posts.

"Dump's closed," I said. "Might as well call it a day."

By the time I pulled into Smitty's Bar & Grill, quite a few pickups lined the gravel.

"Gimme a Bud."

"Make that two," Joey said.

The windowless room was dim and cool. It felt good after being out in the heat all day. Joey had dropped quarters in the juke box, and now Waylon Jennings sang about Luchenbach, Texas.

I swung around on my bar stool. A group of old men were playing dominoes in a back corner. Joey had joined a group playing shuffleboard along the other wall, opposite the door.

"Nothing like that first beer when you're hot and thirsty," I said to the man sitting on the bar stool next to me.

"Well, you got to keep trying."

"I do. Second, third, fourth . . . It just ain't the same."

"Just like your first time, but that don't mean you're gonna stop."

"Stop what?" Joey asked, coming up to the bar for another beer."

"Stopping ain't even in your vocabulary," I said.

"You got that right." Joey flashed a grin and headed back to the shuffleboard.

After a while, a few couples came in, most heading to the back room for hamburgers. Old Lady Divine, erect even with her cane, entered with her middle-aged daughter. I could see Joey keeping an eye out.

The door swung open again and George and Jolene came in, George looking straight ahead. Jolene looked over toward Joey just far enough so that she could turn her back on him before their eyes met, and then marched into the back room side by side with George, head held high and blonde hair swinging.

"Good thing Angie don't work here," Joey's shuffleboard partner remarked after Jolene and George had gone into the rear room. "You trying to get it both ways."

"Hell, I'll get it every way I can," Joey said, and they all laughed.

More people were coming in the door now. City Councilman Tommy Lee and his wife, County Commissioner Billy Bruce and his wife and his wife's parents.

"We need a table for six," Tommy Lee said.

I finished my beer, then headed for the bathrooms in the back. Old Lady Divine and her daughter sat at a small table not far from the big one where the party of six were sitting down.

"Tommy Lee," Old Lady Divine said, motioning him to come over.

"Good evening, Miz Divine. How are you?"

"Tommy Lee, I've known you since you were a child. I knew your mother. A fine woman. What are you doing associating with the likes of that man?"

"Well, ma'm, I . . ."

"Don't you know he's trying to destroy this county? Tearing up the land to build roads that nobody wants or needs, paving over this good blackland God gave us to cherish."

"Well, ma'm, Handler Road will give folks on this end of the county another route to the interstate."

"All seven people out at Jackrabbit Hill? You had better study your geography, young man. As for him, you need to pick better associates."

Mrs. Divine's daughter leaned forward. "Mother, the commissioner will hear you."

"I hope he does. That man needs to put the welfare of the people he represents before his own selfish desires."

"Always good to see you, Miz Divine, Miss Divine," Tommy Lee said, backing away.

Joey and I had started on our burgers and fries when Billy Bruce and his group came out of the back room. Billy Bruce was a big man with a square face, strongly built, but carrying a lot of excess weight. He didn't look our way. Tommy Lee nodded as he held the door for the others.

"What happened to Billy Bruce? He don't look too happy," Joey said.

I told him.

"You don't mess with Miz Divine," Joey said, throwing his head back and laughing. "I never will forget the time I stole some peaches from her orchard. Never again."

He was still smiling when we stepped out into the warm dark night.

A few weeks later, we had to go to the western end of the county to pick up some steel pipe. Most of the crops were in and the fields bare. On the pastureland, black Brangus and white Charolais grazed quietly. The grass looked sparse and dry.

I made a detour to see how Handler Road was coming along. Joey looked at the scraped and bulldozed land and didn't say anything, didn't say anything most of the way back.

The wind picked up, and there was a hint of freshness in the air.

"Looks like we might get some rain," Joey said, brightening up.

A few drops of rain spattered the windshield just as we came into town, but soon stopped. The front had moved to the east; somewhere, somebody was getting a good rain. But here the sidewalks steamed under the hot afternoon sun until no trace of moisture was left.

"Drop me off at Angie's," Joey said. "I'll meet you at Rosalita's later."

By the time I finished running errands, it was later than usual when I arrived at Rosalita's. The County guys were just finishing their supper, and a waitress I hadn't seen before was handing them the check.

"Where's Joey?" I asked, joining the table and signaling the waitress for a beer.

"He took Angie home. Billy Bruce stuck his head in here looking for Tommy Lee, and she just fell apart."

I looked blank.

"You know Handler Road's coming right through her family's place. Gonna have to tear down her mom's house. Or move it, but it ain't worth moving."

"Her mother's lived her whole life there, wouldn't move even after her husband died," another of the men said. "Angie's brother Doug—they're my cousins—farms it, but Angie's mother still keeps chickens and tends the garden, cans every year. Cooks Doug a big old dinner every noon during the week. Just like when he was a kid, Doug says. He can't talk about it in front of his wife, because she lost her mother. While his wife is at work, grabbing fast food, Doug is visiting with his mother over good home cooking. Says he can work twice as hard on that kind of food."

"When Angie saw Billy Bruce, she just started crying and couldn't stop," the first man said. "Told Joey it would kill her mother to move. That farm is her life."

"You should have seen the look on Joey's face," said the third man, who hadn't spoken before.

By the time I finished a plate of tacos, not many people were left at Rosalita's, but I wasn't in the mood to go home.

The Purple Rose was crowded and the jukebox was loud. I grabbed a beer at the bar and felt at home in the dim light and smoky air. Joined the pool players in the next room and made a night of it.

Who is banging on my door, I wondered, stumbling out of bed and into a pair of jeans.

"Yeah," I said.

"Need to talk to you, Bill," Patrolman Jim Fitzgerald said. "Where were you last night?"

"Purple Rose."

"That's not one of your regular places."

"Man's got a right to try something different every once in a while."

"Where's Joey?"

"Don't know."

"Y'all usually together."

"Yeah, well, Joey's got lots of girlfriends."

"Don't I know it. Done talked to 'em. They ain't saying nothing neither."

Wasn't a lot later that I got the call. Patrolman Fitzgerald was just interviewing Joey when I got to the police station."

"You the one that beat up Billy Bruce?"

"Hell, yes," Joey said. "Don't you wish it had been you?"

Policeman Fitzgerald's wife's folks own a farm that the next leg of Handler Road is going to cut through.

The metal door clanged as Jim Fitzgerald shut it behind me.

Joey looked at me, one eye purple and swollen shut, his lips busted.

"Hey," he said.

"Police treating you okay?"

"Sure."

"You don't look so good."

"Got the mother of all hangovers. Couldn't help it. Everybody kept buying me rounds after I took care of Billy Bruce."

"He must outweigh you a hundred pounds, but you hurt him bad."

"Aw, Billy Bruce is tough."

“He don’t look so tough lying up in that hospital bed.”

“Yeah, old lard belly done got soft.”

“Joey, you can’t beat up all of ‘em who are tearing up the countryside.”

“Yeah? Well, maybe, maybe not,” Joey said, his busted lips twisted in a crooked grin. “But I done made a good start.”

Smitty's Bar & Grill

For five years I never left the house. Always a mop or a broom in my hand, a child clinging to my skirt. My husband cried when the last one grew up and moved out.

You think we have a good marriage? Well, it wasn't always that way. Drinking, staying out late with his friends. Never at home when he was needed.

So why did I stay? The children. Always the children. They had to be provided for. They needed a daddy, too. But I knew better. I didn't feel anything for him then.

He's changed now. It's okay. I haven't told many how it happened.

She hesitated, fingering the black fringe of the blue and green shawl draped over the beige couch back. The little wood frame house was still. The two women, sitting at either end of the couch, faced each other, their empty coffee cups resting on coasters on top of the glass coffee table. A few houses down, a dog barked, and a neighbor's screen door slammed. Farther up the street, the school bus had stopped to let off children, their voices and laughter faint in the distance.

"Mama, please let me go."

"Okay, but you have to do exactly what I say."

"I will, I will."

Rosa looked intently into the mirror and applied dark red lipstick. She tilted her head to insert gold hoop earrings; touched up lustrous black hair. Examined the carefully painted nails on hands that had spent years in diaper pails, years washing dishes, years wringing out mops.

She smoothed down her dark red skirt over the small plump body and picked up a black purse to go with her black heels. She glanced into the front bedroom and told the older children to have their homework done before she got back.

Graciela said nothing, large dark eyes fixed on her mother.

She followed close on Rosa's heels, and once outside, climbed into the Chevrolet sedan and fastened her seat belt without being told.

Rosa backed out carefully. The streets were quiet, most families in for the evening. She drove south, taking the pot-holed back streets until she reached the highway heading west out of town, then turned right and drove half a mile.

His pickup was parked in front of Smitty's. She pulled around to the far side of the gravel lot by the side of the dark unpainted building, the neon sign brightly lit: Smitty's Bar & Grill.

"Get in the back seat and lie down so nobody can see you. And don't move."

Graciela obediently crawled over the seat and slid down. Rosa locked all the doors. She took a deep breath and started across the gravel.

She hesitated just a moment before the unpainted wooden door, took another deep breath, then pulled hard on the handle, and walked right in. Her heels clicked like castanets on the wooden floor. She stepped up to the bar and climbed onto a stool. Her feet dangled above the floor.

The light in this front room was dim and the air heavy with smoke. On the wall behind the bar, a neon chuck wagon, pulled by stout horses with flashing hooves, rolled endlessly, going nowhere.

"Bring me a beer, please."

"What kind?" asked the bartender.

Rosa paused, looking at the bottles lined up on the shelf.

"It doesn't matter. Any kind."

She stared at the creamy foam topping the amber liquid in the chilled mug. It was all she could do not to make a face as she swallowed the bitter fluid. She paused, then sipped again.

Country western played on the jukebox. A few stools to her right sat a man with red hair covering his sunburnt, heavily muscled arm, lifting a schooner of beer.

No one sat on her left. On this weekday night, only a few of the tables were filled. Her husband and his friends sat at a table against the back wall, talking quietly, empty bottles lined up before them.

She took another sip. Soft laughter and the murmur of conversation drifted up from the tables. She sipped again and waited.

She heard the scrape of a chair pushed backwards and slow footsteps. She looked straight ahead and sipped again.

He came up on her left.

"Rosa, this is not you," he said quietly.

"This is the new me," she said, not turning around.

"Rosa, this is not who you are. Please go home to the children."

"You're talking about the old me. You're looking at the new me."

"Rosa, you don't belong here, not in this kind of place. You belong at home with the children."

"You might as well get used to the new me. This is where I'll be from now on.

She took another swallow of beer and stared straight ahead. He paused, helpless, then retreated. She gazed steadily at the neon horses and endlessly rolling wagon wheels.

The clink of falling quarters was audible, then Kenny Rogers' music filled the spaces in the small room.

She traced a line along the side of the cool moist glass with a red-lacquered fingertip. Tiny bubbles rose through the pale liquid to the top, and the foamy head disappeared.

The man to her right dangled a cigarette between thick fingers; the red hair on his wrist tangled in his watch band. Smoke drifted up toward the ceiling.

The bartender wiped the left end of the bar with a damp cloth. Kenny Rogers crooned there was a time to play your hand and a time to fold your cards. The horses' hooves flashed and the wheels rolled.

She heard footsteps and then the voice of her husband's best friend.

"Rosa, I've known you a long time. You've never been to a place like this. You know how Benny feels seeing you sitting here. Won't you go home?"

"The new me goes to places like this."

She took a sip of warmish beer, listened to the retreating footsteps.

Two men at another table ordered more beer. The man at the bar lit another cigarette and slowly blew a plume of blue smoke into the stale air. And on the jukebox, Johnny Rodriguez sang of love.

More footsteps, and then her husband's voice.

"Rosa, please go home. It's not right for you to be here. You're not the sort of person to leave the children and go out like this."

"That's the old me. Now I go anyplace."

The unpainted door swung open. Two young men in jeans and boots walked up to the bar and sat on Rosa's left. A worn circle in the hip pocket of one, the denim faded a lighter color, showed the outlines of a can of Red Man.

The liquid notes of Willie's "Whiskey River" poured from the jukebox. Smoke coiled and drifted upward, disappearing into a dim haze.

She heard returning footsteps. Then a long silence.

She studied the rows of bottles behind the bar. The neon hooves flashed in place and the chuck wagon wheels turned and turned. Willie crooned "Blue Eyes Crying in the

Rain."

"Rosa . . ."

She looked at her polished nails, the softened cuticles, approved the deep rich red and oval shapes.

"Rosa," he began again. "If I go home, will you?"

"Yes," she said.

There's not many I've told that to. We get along now. I don't cook like I used to when the children were all home. H.E.B. tortillas are good enough. But when the boys came over the other night I made my own. "Please, Mama," they said the day before, so I did. Afterwards my husband said, "How come you cook for the boys but not for me?" "Because those are *my* boys," I said. "They're *mine*. You can get a husband around any corner."

Birthright

Perhaps it was because the wind was from the south, the first morning with the smell of spring. Or perhaps his mind had simply drifted back until it found an anchor. He had stayed the night at his office, gazing out at the city lights, smoking too many cigarettes. He finally dozed toward morning, but started at intervals, heart racing, an edge of panic forcing him into wakefulness.

Pain seemed preferable to this inner hysteria. You never understood, he thought, how the almost invisible daily routines held you from the abyss—until they were gone. Sleeping in the same bed, waking to the smell of coffee and the play of their daughters, bright as the morning. Even when he was raging against the fierce tensions and bitter disappointments. At least the ground had seemed firm under his feet.

When he had let himself out on the street, still shaky from the long night, he tried to focus on the familiar outlines, the double line of buildings shaping the sky. Like the woods he had grown up in: this much sky and no more. Perhaps it was that, or maybe it was the breeze, intimating spring. He raised his head, breathing in quickly, like a drowsing dog suddenly startled by an elusive scent.

Out of habit, he bought a paper, then found it useful as a screen as he sat in a diner sipping coffee. For the first time in years, memory overtook him. He let it happen, drifting back without resistance. Smoke curled in the air, and the ash on his cigarette lengthened.

"Billy," his mother called from the kitchen, as he snuggled deeper into the hollow his small body had worn in the old mattress. The air was just crisp enough to make the warmth of his bed luxurious.

The rich smell of brewing coffee, the aroma of yeast-risen hotcakes and sizzling bacon, pulled him to his knees. He stepped gingerly onto the cool floor, then danced across the room, through the kitchen and out the back door into the colorless pre-dawn light. The smell of wood smoke was like incense in the morning air.

Bobby was already on his way back from the outhouse—or from the direction of it.

"You wash your hands?" their mother asked, hearing them on the porch.

"Yes'm," in unison, as William reached guiltily for the pitcher, conscientiously washing up while Bobby wiggled his fingers in the basin and then wiped his dry face with the towel.

Baby Julie was already in her highchair, banging on the tray with a spoon. Their father was just emerging from the bedroom. The creak of the loose back step as it bore his father's full weight was as much a part of William's morning as the smell of coffee and bacon.

"You wait for your father," his mother said sharply as Bobby reached toward the bacon.

Suddenly William was aware of his own vast hunger. The platter of hotcakes steamed, and at the bottom was a little yellow pool where rivulets of butter had dribbled down the edges. Next to it stood the pitcher of rich dark sorghum. At the other end of the table there was a platter of thick-sliced bacon flanked by a big pitcher of milk, all foamy on top.

William didn't think he could hold out.

After an eternity, his father returned. He sat in his place at the head of the table, then paused. His mother's stern gaze lowered Bobby's head along with the rest.

Fortunately, the blessing was short—William's father was hungry, too.

At first William ate quickly, then paused dreamily to savor each bite. Bobby ate rapidly until sated, then fidgeted restlessly util he was allowed to leave the table. Baby Julie happily crammed bites of hotcake into her mouth with both hands.

William's father held out his cup for more coffee. His wife, anticipating him, was already at the stove, pot in hand.

A spasm, as though his temples had contracted, brought William abruptly back to the dingy diner, the fallen cigarette ash. He rubbed his head, bewildered, feeling as though something had eluded him.

A young waitress, misinterpreting his sudden questing look, slowly sauntered over.

"Something else?"

"More coffee, please," William said, smiling up at her, buying time. For a moment, his attention was caught by her regular features, thin brown hair, and sallow complexion. Still, there was something of the vitality of youth about her, he thought, in spite of the sickly look of the city.

But when she returned with the coffee, he sat staring at it for a moment, realizing he had lost the thread, whatever it was.

On the street outside, the fragile scent of spring had been crushed by diesel and gas fumes. The mechanical throb of the city blotted out all other rhythms. For one wild instant, William had a double image of himself, one superimposed on the other. He saw himself standing there on a dirty street in the middle of the early morning roar of traffic, scraps of paper and other refuse blown in little eddies, while the tall buildings seemed to grow taller, pressing against him and stifling him. At the same time, he saw himself a small boy having strayed farther than he had intended into the deep pine woods; suddenly panicked and suffocated with fear.

William felt light-headed, free-floating, as though he might put his foot down and find nothing there. He shook himself lightly, like a horse shivering off an unreachable fly.

I've got to get my mind on my work, he thought. But instead, as he walked briskly down the street, he remembered with a smile how he had found his way back home out of the woods—it really hadn't been very far. And had run straight to his mother, thrown himself at her. She had held him against her full breast, gently rocking him, saying nothing. She knew. She always knew.

Suddenly William was flooded with contentment, like an infant rocked in a cradle. For a moment he was insulated from the street.

And then bitterness swept over him. Overwhelmed him. He had no wife to go home to. No home to go home to. Gayle had kicked him out. He walked faster, striding vengefully down the pavement.

It was the usual time when he reached the office. In the elevator he had surreptitiously touched up his hair, straightened his tie, and he thought he walked into the main office with his usual casual ease.

"Good morning," Jan said brightly, and he returned her smile with his customary good morning.

When he walked into his own office, he noticed—as ordinarily he probably wouldn't have—that Jan had emptied the overfilled ash trays and gathered up the dirty coffee cups.

He liked his office. It wasn't opulent, but it was handsome and well-furnished, with a comfortable, almost homey air. It was the only home he had, he thought suddenly, the bitterness rising again.

William settled into his desk chair as though into a familiar groove. Almost immediately the phone rang, then Jan came in. Soon he was immersed in his day. Familiar irritations gave him stability.

In the course of the day, William found himself cataloging abrasions: the transparent racism of one of his clients, the ruthless intra-office jockeying of the other young lawyers, the frustration of a thousand trivial interruptions. The hurt and bitterness almost overwhelmed him as he realized what he was doing. How was a man to live if he had no one to go home to?

For a moment the picture rose before his eyes. He saw himself, face drawn with the strain of the day, drop wearily onto the elegant couch.

"Oh, baby, what's the matter?" Gayle would say, stroking his head. "Lemme fix you a drink."

"Daddy, Daddy," his two little girls would cry, climbing over him for a minute before Gayle set them to play in another room.

Then Gayle would sit beside him, long legs crossed at the knee, while he told her about his day.

When he thought about his loss, bitterness and confusion ate into him. He was not like other men. He never stormed in, taking out an ugly rage on his wife and children. Like his father had done.

He remembered his father coming home from the sawmill, some days laughing the deep rich laugh that seemed to bubble up from some inner fountain. Rough-housing with William and Bobby, scooping them up like footballs and making a broken-field run.

But some days he came in sullen and grim, and the boys got out of his way, scurrying around the corner of the house as though a dark cloud of fear had suddenly covered the sun. On those days he would storm into the house, finding fault with everything their mother had and hadn't done. He never touched her, though. That was an unspoken law between them. As he raged and criticized, she never said a word, but the lines of her face grew haughtier, and visible willpower outlined her body. When he was spent, she would walk stiffly out of the room and shut herself into the bedroom.

"Dumb nigger! Who he think he is!"

And William would hear the old pine dresser rattle until he thought every drawer would fall out.

THUMP!

CRASH!

WHAM!

And William would visualize each piece of furniture as it hit the floor or the walls.

"Think he the only one around here that work."

THUMP!

"Black ass laying up in the bed every morning."

CRASH!

"Hunh! Fault-finding me!"

WHAM!

"Dumb nigger!"

SLAM!

Eventually there would be silence, and William would picture his mother standing disheveled in the middle of the bedroom, sweat dripping from her face. But in a little while, she would come out, shiny black hair carefully in place, her face smooth and softened.

Then his mother would go about cooking supper on the wood stove, lifting great black cast-iron skillets of cornbread with one hand. Talking easily to his father. Finally beginning to hum a little as she moved into the rhythm of the work.

The rhythm of the work. For a moment William looked around him at the piles of paper on his desk, heard the carping tones of one of the other lawyers complaining to Jan. His gorge rose.

When finally he left the office, the weather had turned bleak and chill. A raw wind swept the dirty pavement, and the setting sun made an eerie glow in the polluted sky. William hurried to a nearby bar.

It was warm and softly lit, filled with the afterwork crowd. He sat at the bar, sipping a double Scotch and glancing at the evening news. After a while, when the crowd began to thin, William felt panicky. He had no place to go. Then he caught hold of himself. He knew a nice little restaurant, not too far, and he could kill some time by walking.

The night air was cool, but the wind had dropped and it was pleasant to be outside. William stretched his long legs, enjoying the movement. The alcohol glowed warm inside him, and the long walk eased the tension of the day.

As he entered the expensive little restaurant, he liked knowing he could walk in and order anything he wanted, the price immaterial.

He dawdled a little over the menu, carefully choosing wine. William was not a gourmet. He took a healthy interest in food, as his slim body indicated, but tonight he was pampering himself, distracting himself. He lingered over his meal, sipping glass after glass of wine, ending with coffee and Drambuie. Still, the evening stretched before him. He considered a movie, but dismissed the idea. It was too cold and lonely.

He decided, ironically, that a singles bar would be fitting. He did not like that sort of thing, but he needed crowds and noise.

For a moment he thought of his brother Bobby who had stayed home, married a hometown girl, and set up his own automobile repair shop. He was on his second marriage, and his girlfriends were notorious, one having a baby the same month as his wife.

I'm not like that, William thought with an inner cry. Unlike other men, he had been faithful to his wife. Once or twice when Gayle was visiting her mother, William had fallen into something at a party. But it hadn't meant anything to him and he had never followed up on it.

He shook his head in the cold air and realized he was mumbling to himself. Hastily, he hailed a cab.

At first he enjoyed the novelty of the bar, steadily sipping his drink and watching the action. It was like being at a play, but with no division between actors and audience —everyone was both. One whole wall was a mirror, and William particularly liked watching the play of eye contact in the mirror—watching someone watch someone. But after a while, repugnance and distaste filled him. He abruptly got to his feet, tossed off the last of his drink, and hurried out the door.

He had drunk heavily, and he had to concentrate carefully on his steps. He took a cab back to the deserted office and carefully let himself into the building.

Safely back in his office, he collapsed on the couch, the room spinning slightly. He thought he had hit it right, gotten himself safely back yet drunk enough to sleep. By an effort, he stilled the room and sank into sleep.

Suddenly, he jerked awake in terror. What was it? Then he remembered.

Sitting straight up on the couch, William began to cry, deep racking sobs that came out of his belly and quivered his shoulders. The sense of loss was like a knife twisting in his guts, and he cried aloud with the pain of it, the whole couch shaking with his shuddering sobs.

"I want my family." And he saw the protected nest, feathered with his two little girls, his wife warm and sensuous in the dark. Need overcame him. He needed a woman. Gayle. His wife.

The next morning William woke early, his throat parched, his head aching, his whole body stiff and sore. Enough of this, he thought, I'm not cut out to be a drunkard. Although the idea of food repelled him, he knew he would feel better if he ate. Hastily he cleaned up in the office bathroom.

Out on the street, the freshness of the day was yet unsullied. Bright sun overlay the morning coolness. William remembered spring mornings in the deep pine woods, the half-mile walk down the red dirt road to the bus stop, a glimpse of squirrels playing tag around the bole of a large pine. Indefinable longings had pulled at him then. He had wanted to bury himself in the beauty of the morning, run after it, press it to him. Sometimes he had pretended he was an Indian, with nothing to do but roam the woods all day. He never did, though; he always climbed aboard the old school bus and rattled down the hardtop to the country school.

William had liked school. Early he had discovered the unknown worlds books opened to him, and he had liked the exercise of his mind. But he was quietly studious and never drew attention to himself in class. He was competent enough in games and sports to be accepted, though he was never outstanding like Bobby. But there had always been a part of William that he kept to himself.

William paused outside the coffee shop for a last breath of the morning. He was still a little shaky but felt better now that he was in motion. He ate a hearty breakfast of scrambled eggs and toast, coffee and juice, and gradually a sense of physical wellbeing began to replace the strung-out feeling. He had always taken pleasure in his smooth brown healthy body, its lithe grace and serenity.

William lingered over his last cup of coffee, thinking. All right, if this was the way it was to be he had to order his life. Rent an apartment. Rearrange his affairs. Dispatch it.

Once he had reached that point, William moved quickly, renting a furnished apartment, expensive, modern, and sterile. He chose a time when he knew Gayle was at work and went by for his personal things.

A wave hit him as he walked in the door, a sense of unreality. Had he ever lived in this place with its deep rugs, its tall potted plants, its carefully tended African violets? As he walked through the apartment, it seemed to breathe Gayle's presence. He looked into the bedroom his daughters shared, with its modest disorder: a few dolls and games lying about, the younger daughter's bed not carefully made. Pain tore at his throat, and he staggered under the hurt. He hastened into what used to be his and Gayle's bedroom, averting his eyes from the king-sized bed that dominated the room, and hurriedly grabbed his clothes out of the closet and dresser drawers. Everything else he left as it was.

It was strange, he thought, how little mark he had made on the apartment. It was as though its life continued to flow on, his absence no more than a ripple. Something nagged at the back of his mind. He frowned, rubbing his head. Finally, as he drove off, he let memories wash over him without trying to understand.

He remembered how he had felt as a boy when his father left. The ache, the empty place left unfilled. And yet, life had gone on very much as before. He still woke to the smell of coffee and bacon and sat down to hearty breakfasts in the early morning light. The order of his day had always been set by his mother. She assigned the chores, saw that they did their lessons, that they washed their faces and hands and combed their hair. None of that changed after his father left.

It had been hard, but they had enough to eat. His mother sold butter and eggs as she had always done, and now she took in laundry, too. She had a huge garden, or at least it seemed enormous to William when he stared the length of the long rows he had to hoe. He could remember times, their hog meat long since eaten up, when his mother would take to the woods with a shotgun, bringing back small game for supper—rabbits, squirrels, birds.

His mother was always busy, but she was never harassed by the work. She sang and whistled about the house, and the tight look was gone from her face.

William's head began to ache, and as he stopped at a red light, he tried to shake away the bafflement.

What had gone wrong between him and Gayle? He knew it had started when she went back to school.

For a moment, he forgot about what it had been like at the end. Everyday unbearable tension, punctuated by violent quarrels. Vibrations of hostility so thick you could have cut them with a knife. Gayle not wanting him to even touch her. His own sullen threats to leave.

Instead, his mind skipped back to the early days of their marriage. He had been a struggling law student, she a secretary. Barely making it on her salary. He remembered hot summer afternoons, weekends, when they had shared a quart of cold beer, mellow music on the radio, playing and giggling until the romping turned passionate. Rhythmic intertwining of two warm brown bodies in the middle of a rumpled bed.

William went suddenly weak inside, remembering.

And the parties. William was so proud when he walked in with Gayle by his side. She was so beautiful with her long slim legs, high full breasts, elastic grace and elegant style. And even later, when he was a new and coming lawyer, going to almost all-white parties, he always felt there wasn't a man in the room who had such a woman.

Deprivation tore at William's insides. Who was she sleeping with now? Lava poured over him. And yet, he knew it wasn't that. She had left him, and not even for another man. Why? Why?

William stopped in front of his new apartment. His head felt as though it might split in two. For a moment he slumped over the steering wheel, his head in his hands. Then he shook himself hard, like a man dazed by an unexpected blow, trying to get his wits back. He rolled out of the car, gathered up his clothes, and ran up the steps to his second floor apartment.

After he had hung up his clothes and put away the underthings, he flopped down on the couch. No T.V. Not even a radio. Sighing, he loosened his tie and thought how nice a hot bath would make him feel. He ran a deep tub of water, got the soap out of his briefcase, and gave himself up to luxury.

Feeling as though he had rinsed away his hurts along with the soapy water, he stepped out of the tub and reached . . . No towel. The goddamn place wasn't as good as a motel. He grabbed up his dirty shirt and dried off the best he could, wadding it up and flinging it in the corner when he was through.

When he had dressed in fresh clothes, he felt better again. He hurried off to the grocery store zipping up and down aisles, throwing things into his cart. This is kind of fun, he thought, remembering how Gayle had grown to loathe grocery shopping.

He paused in the housewares section, wondering what to get. Until he married Gayle, William had always lived in dormitories or cheap boarding houses, and had never given much thought to outfitting a kitchen. However, he knew there wasn't much to it. He grabbed up some pots and pans, thought he'd get paper plates and plastic ware to tide him over for a while.

On impulse, he bought a cast iron skillet. It wasn't't black, though, like his mother's had been. The instructions glued to the middle explained how to season it, and William had a sudden revelation. In imagination he saw the big black skillets and the great cast iron pot his mother used for so many things: boiling clothes, making soap, rendering lard, making hominy. They had not always been like that, as in his childish mind it had seemed. Into their roughened black outsides and their smooth, shiny black insides had gone years of endless repetition of the days' tasks—the rhythm of a life. William looked at the metallic new skillet, a circle of paper glued to its center, and his throat tightened with a sense of loss. Somewhere, somehow, he had missed something.

That night William lay huddled on his new bed, unwashed sheets smelling like department store. Images spun through his mind: Gayle singing to herself while she cooked supper, the two little girls carefully setting the table; Gayle dressing to go out, trying the effect of new gold hoop earrings. All the beauty and order of their life together. How could she have done this to him? William wept.

He remembered the time after his father was gone, when his mother had become even more involved in the church. One night he had lain awake and the cold dark had seemed empty yet menacing with his mother gone. Bobby was sound asleep beside him and he could hear Julie's light even breathing, but he couldn't sleep. In the night silence, he imagined stealthy footfalls. He huddled closer to Bobby, who was oblivious, sunk in the sleep of healthy exhaustion. After an eternity, he heard a distant car, then the sound of its door closing, goodbyes called. He heard his mother's sure step as she made her way in the dark, padded about her room readying herself for bed. He heard her sigh as the bed creaked with her weight, and the sigh seemed to come straight from his heart as he settled himself next to Bobby and fell instantly asleep.

A kaleidoscope of images whirled through William's head, attacking him, confusing him until he couldn't tell when he was asleep and dreaming, when awake and tormented by memories. He struggled under the weight of memory like a drowning man whose frantic and violent efforts simply re-submerge him.

At last, exhausted, he fell asleep just before morning, the unaccustomed tenseness finally seeping out of his long, slim, graceful body. He must have begun to dream, for as he slowly awoke to the morning light, it seemed to him that Gayle was in the kitchen, hot biscuits in the oven, the two little girls well-scrubbed with their hair carefully braided. Just like every other morning. Some unease nagged at him, but he couldn't remember what was wrong.

Then he awoke to the stale morning light and the nauseating smell of his department store sheets. Self-pity washed over him. Suddenly he straightened, furious. I'm not going to live this way, he shouted, slamming his fist on the bed. The bitch! If that's what she wanted, then she could have it. He was the one making all the money. There were other women in the world.

He stormed into the kitchen, carefully measured the coffee into the filter, poured the water into the top of the coffee maker.

In the bathroom, he kicked the wadded-up dirty shirt he had once dried with. Christ, he thought as it unrolled, What is that crap? He looked more closely and discovered the discoloring mildew all over the once-white shirt. He picked it up and hurled it into the wastebasket.

That afternoon, William took off from work early and went on a reckless buying spree. So he didn't have a wife. He'd make himself comfortable.

That night, he turned on his new color T.V., broiled a thick steak, poured himself a glass of Beaujolais. He ate slowly, savoring the meat, the tossed salad. The noise of the T.V. filled the empty spaces in the slick new room.

William pushed aside his plate, lit a cigarette, and leaned back against the cream-colored couch. He took a long sip of his wine, thinking.

When Gayle had started back to school, it wasn't long before she began insisting that he help around the house. Little things, really. Perhaps he should have done more.

William slowly exhaled a thin cloud of cigarette smoke. He wondered now why he had resisted so. At the time, he had felt that since he worked hard all day, he ought to be able to relax in his own home. It hadn't been so bad at first, but when Gayle wanted to go on to graduate school, it had become harder and harder.

He took another sip of wine, idly fingering the glass

in his hand. At first he had bathed and put the girls to bed on the nights Gayle had classes. Read to them. Told them stories.

For a moment, his throat tightened—remembering the two little girls in their cotton nightgowns, pulling on his arms, teasing him. "Tell us what it was like when you were a little boy, Daddy." He remembered how he had sat wondering how to tell two little girls living in a high rise apartment, fully climate conditioned, what it was like to live in an unpainted cabin in the piney woods. How did you explain that the weather is not a man on T.V. making marks on a screen, but a presence in your life: icy board floors on a winter morning, warm living sunshine like a friendly arm across your back, steady rain turning the red clay slick and squishing in your shoes?

Somehow, unaccountably, he remembered cold winter nights and icy sheets, his mother warming bricks in the oven and wrapping them in flannel to keep his feet warm. For a moment, images of his mother arose before him: brewing her home-made cough remedies, poulticing an infected place, baking bread. All the unobtrusive details of everyday life. As though she held his life in her hands.

William began to rub his head again, the ache about the temples. Really, it wasn't so much that Gayle had asked him to do some work about the house. He had always worked hard. It wasn't that. Why had it made him so angry?

Again, William had the feeling that something just out of reach was eluding him.

He finished the wine and set the empty glass on the coffee table next to his plate. The steak grease had congealed around the edges of the meat scraps, cold and white, mingling with the stale smell of cigarette ash where he had stubbed out his cigarette in the thickening grease.

The T.V. blared.

The next morning William awoke tired and sluggish. Over toast and coffee, he decided to get out more. He girded himself for the day by planning his strategy. He had to meet new people.

The following Saturday evening he walked into a friend's apartment, carefully dressed, a little excited. Harry welcomed him loudly, drew him into the kitchen to an improvised bar. William felt a little steadier with a Scotch in his hand. He didn't know many people, but Harry took him round for introductions, always mentioning the firm William was with. Watching the women, William felt the power his position gave him—it felt good.

After a while, William found himself on the couch taking a toke and passing the joint to the woman who sat next to him. She was vibrant with the health and vigor of youth, and it had been a long time since he had heard so thick an accent—the words sliding from vowel to vowel, the consonants indistinct. It reminded him of home, and he looked more closely at the young woman. She had the firm, ripe, full-to-bursting look of robust youth, and her body moved freely and naturally.

William took another long pull as the joint came round, and felt himself mellowing out. Into the music. Into the dark rich warmth of the voices all around him. He turned to the woman—Pam—asked her about herself.

Later in the evening, a group of them went out dancing. Afterwards, he and Pam returned to his apartment. They undressed quickly, and William buried his face in the full, smooth brown breasts, need almost overwhelming him. Body against body in a steady rhythmic beat, and all else blotted out. Afterwards, William fell asleep curled round her back, one hand clutching a full ripe breast.

Toward morning, William awoke and saw her in deep repose, but the soft young curves of her body were not Gayle, and a kind of desperation rose up in him.

Monday, William was back at his office, glad he had the safety of that structure. He threw himself even more deeply into his work, voluntarily working late nights. Sometimes he dined out, came home late and fell into bed. Other evenings he took pride in cooking for himself, and dined with the T.V.

The weekends were harder. As often as he could, he went to parties, slept late.

One evening, William found himself over at Pam's apartment. He and Harry had brought the liquor; it was a Friday night, half a dozen people drifting in.

It was a modest two-bedroom apartment, part of a large complex, one of those carpeted, centrally heated and cooled, motel-like apartments. He could guess what luxury it represented to Pam, and he could see the care with which she had decorated it. She was a waitress in one of the better restaurants. Hard work, but she made a living for herself and her son.

There was a Nancy Wilson record on the stereo, and a group were playing cards at the dinette table. Some of the women made a blenderful of strawberry daiquiris and set out a bowl of chips. Soon a few people began to dance in the small living room. The card players laughed and cracked jokes.

For a long while, William stood to one side, watching, but eventually began to dance with Pam, his long slim body tuned to the music. It was Michael Jackson, and William let his body go, moving freely, imaginatively, to the surface beat of the music. Underneath, a deeper, throbbing beat seemed to unite their two separated bodies, as though they were joined by an invisible chord.

Pam put the Commodores on the stereo, and pressed against him, her soft warm body enveloping him. After a while, he asked if he could stay the night.

In the warm dark of the bedroom, William marveled at the lushness of the body before him. He suckled the soft full breasts, and a kind of peace descended on him even though his body trembled. He kissed her stomach, inching his way lower and lower in rhythm with her soft moans. He paused . . . then pressed his face into the moist silken warmth, his tongue questing through intricate layers.

Dark pine forests hidden from the moonlight. Lovers' moans. Wind shuddering in the branches high overhead. A convulsive gasp.

She grabbed him by the shoulders.

"Turn over, honey."

William lay back, cradled in the big bed. Slowly She descended on him, gliding downward, cushioning him in Her yielding warmth. William melted. And then, an electrifying squeeze. William cried aloud. Rhythmically She rose and fell. Pausing. Squeezing. Moving forward and back. She played with his body.

The world disappeared and William drifted into eternity, floating above time and space. Then waves began to build, like pounding surf. He tossed on the turbulence, crying aloud in the gushing warmth. Then stilled in the enormous calm.

The next morning, Pam woke him up and made him

get dressed early. He was seated at the dinette table before her two-year-old son woke up.

"He know I have friends," she said, "but he never gonna see a man in bed with me unless that man be around."

William sat sipping a cup of coffee while Pam cooked him a good old-fashioned breakfast, as she called it: bacon and eggs, hash browns and biscuits. She babied him, teasing and petting him.

For an instant, an image of her life rose before him: on her feet all day, taking orders in her carefully pressed uniform.

Tony came walking into the kitchen, a mannish little fellow, and Pam introduced him to William. William smiled at the obvious delight Pam took in her son. It was a pretty picture. She was laughing and hugging him, then setting him down, saying, "Now you get on in there to the table while I get this breakfast."

Pam's eyes were shining as she set the big country breakfast before him. He could feel her aching for a man, a father for her son, could feel how desperately she wanted to quit her job and stay home—in her own home, making a nest. William knew he mustn't do this again.

He watched her laughing and kidding, joking and babying him. For a moment, it was as though he had double vision. The image of his mother's warm kitchen rose before him at the same time that he saw Pam, vital yet wistful, hardly more than a child playing with her child. William felt desperately lonesome, almost faint with the intensity.

"What's the matter, baby?" Pam asked, reaching out and taking his hand.

"Nothing," he said, brushing his hand across his forehead. "Probably that last daiquiri," he added, smiling.

As soon as he could, William left. He had lots of work, he said. Tony had turned on the T.V. and was half watching the Saturday morning cartoons while he rolled a little toy car along the edge of the coffee table.

"Bye," he said, glancing up as William left.

William kept his resolution, staying away from parties where he might meet Pam. She was a sweet, simple girl, but that was all. He was not about to get deeply involved with her, and for her sake he'd better stop seeing her for good. Instead, he threw himself into his work, driving himself night after night.

He began to suffer from insomnia, and although he was exhausted, he slept fitfully if at all. Once after a restless, tormented night, he slipped into a deep sleep just before morning.

He dreamed he was walking in the pasture near his childhood home, a surreal, shifting landscape in the dream. The pasture was much larger than in reality, and the woods were barely visible in the distance. He was crossing the pasture, trying to get back home to his mother. There was an urgency, but he couldn't remember why. He began walking faster, but the landscape kept changing. He saw a bare and leafless sweet gum that was a landmark, but the ground dipped down, covered by grass withered and pale, and he lost sight of the tree.

Then the scene changed. He was in the yard outside the house, and there was a big party. People were laughing and talking all around him. There was something he needed to tell Gayle, but every time he tried to reach her, someone else pulled her aside.

William woke abruptly. Again he was overpowered

by the feeling that some kind of understanding was just beyond his reach. He lay still for a moment, letting the dream wash over him.

His bed was soft and luxurious, and he felt enclosed by it. He buried his face in the big fluffy pillow and snuggled deep into the warmth generated by his own body. He let his mind go blank and he lay quiet, feeling the life gently vibrating through his body. His breathing was slow and even. Finally, images began to arise.

He saw an infant, pillowed against large breasts, and he felt a gentle rocking, as though he were floating on the sea. Warmth enclosed him like a cocoon. Sweet peace and contentment flooded him, and the very surface of his skin felt alive.

William felt the presence of his mother.

The light grew stronger in the room, and the sound of the traffic more insistent. Gradually William sat up and swung his long legs over the side of the bed.

As he showered, his mind drifted back to his high school years. The long days of work and study, his retreat deeper into his books. Bobby and Julie loud in the heat of school activities and social life. His mother's strong presence over them all. When they graduated, she gave each in turn their third of the money his father had contributed through the years.

He was struck now, thinking of how she had kept the money safe for them all those years, never touching a penny. She had supported her children by herself, raising them alone to adulthood. Day after day, she had fed them, clothed them, sheltered them. And by the time they were grown, their father's money was as much their mother's gift as their father's. William was stunned, remembering.

He dressed slowly, as in a daze, fumbling through

his morning chores. At the office, he smiled at Jan, and it was as though he were seeing her face for the first time. He noticed the deceptively simple, expensive cut of her hair, the carefully applied make-up. For the first time, he wondered what her inward life was like.

Once at the privacy of his desk, he buried his face in his hands, leaning his elbows on the polished grain of the oak. He had always prided himself on his own consideration toward Jan, but he was perfectly aware that she had to put up with the assholes in the office.

Gayle had been a secretary. What had her life been like? His phone rang, and then Jan drew his attention to a deadline, and soon he was immersed in his day.

But that night, the nagging questions returned. Again he recalled Gayle's return to school. He could understand her wanting a more challenging job. He sympathized. But as she began to work in earnest on a doctorate in psychology, she seemed to be slipping away from him, as though her attention were elsewhere. And he deeply resented it.

She had always been a good mother, and she continued to be. When she started back to school, *he* was the one who got scanted.

For a moment, the image of his mother rose before him. Sitting on the three-legged stool, the milk zinging into the pail. The garden fecund under her hands. The warm kitchen, a deep dish of blackberry cobbler, purple-red under the crust, cooling underneath the window.

Pine-scented evenings, a new moon rising above the treetops. The deep hush of midnight.

His mother and the nurturing earth.

And where was his father? For a moment, the walls receded, the floor dropped from beneath his feet, and

William thought his head would explode in the sudden vacuum.

A hive of connected memories swarmed him.

He remembered once when the preacher had come to dinner with them. Afterwards, leaning back from the supper table, he had turned to William's mother.

"You've done right well for yourself, Miz Johnson, without a man."

"Hunh! What I need a man for?"

Once in the early years of his marriage, William had come home to find several of Gayle's friends in a heated discussion.

"Men are good for nothing but fucking!" he heard one say.

When he opened the door, someone said, "Speaking of the devil," and they all laughed easily.

William got up and walked around the room, shaking himself and holding his head.

He remembered the increasing number of quarrels he and Gayle were having toward the end. It seemed to him that the less he saw of her, the more she demanded of him. He began coming and going as he pleased, and he would come home to find friends of hers staying with the girls while Gayle was at class. Finally, after one heated quarrel, she told him to get out. He was simply in her way.

Again, William felt completely adrift, without anchor. For the first time in years, the memory rose stark and clear:

The summer heat pressed against the interior of the cabin like the hot breath of a sick animal. His father was in an ugly mood. He had been laid off from the mill for a few days, and the tension had risen with the heat. The children made themselves scarce, but William's mother had gone about her chores as usual. Eventually, William's father began shouting at her, becoming more and more abusive while she rinsed turnip greens in the sink. Her body stiffened, but she continued to trim and dice the turnips with her usual care. The steady rhythmic slicing seemed to infuriate him.

"By god, woman, look at me when I'm talking to you!" he shouted.

She carefully put her knife down, wiped her hands on her apron, and turned slowly, deliberately, towards him. Such a look was in her eyes that for a moment he hesitated. Then in a rage he shouted, "Black bitch! Don't you look at me like that."

Just as deliberately, she turned back to her turnips and began slicing them. With her back to him, she seemed as solid and unmovable as a rock.

In fury and despair, he put his hand on her—*put his hand on her*—grabbed her by the shoulder as though to jerk her toward him. She turned of her own accord then and he read it in her eyes.

Blustering, he stormed out of the house.

William's mother lifted the greens out of the sink and dropped them into the boiling water along with the diced turnips and slices of fatback. She carefully placed the cover on the heavy pot.

William pressed against the wall, bare foot rubbing against a bare leg. His mother went into the bedroom and began pulling clothes out of the closet and dresser, muttering to herself. "Knowed better than lay a hand on me. Told him so at the beginning."

That night when William's father returned, all his things were sitting on the front porch. When he saw them, he took them and left.

His father had left. Ceased to exist.

William fell back across his bed, faint. The room spun round and round and there was a roaring in his ears. He felt himself slipping away. For a few minutes he gave in to the terror, gasping and writhing on the bed. Finally he stilled, clutching a pillow and panting a little.

After a while, he went into the bathroom and washed his face. He straightened his tie in the mirror, then went back into the bedroom. He flipped through his address book, dialed a number.

"Hello, Pam? Hey, how're you doing . . ."

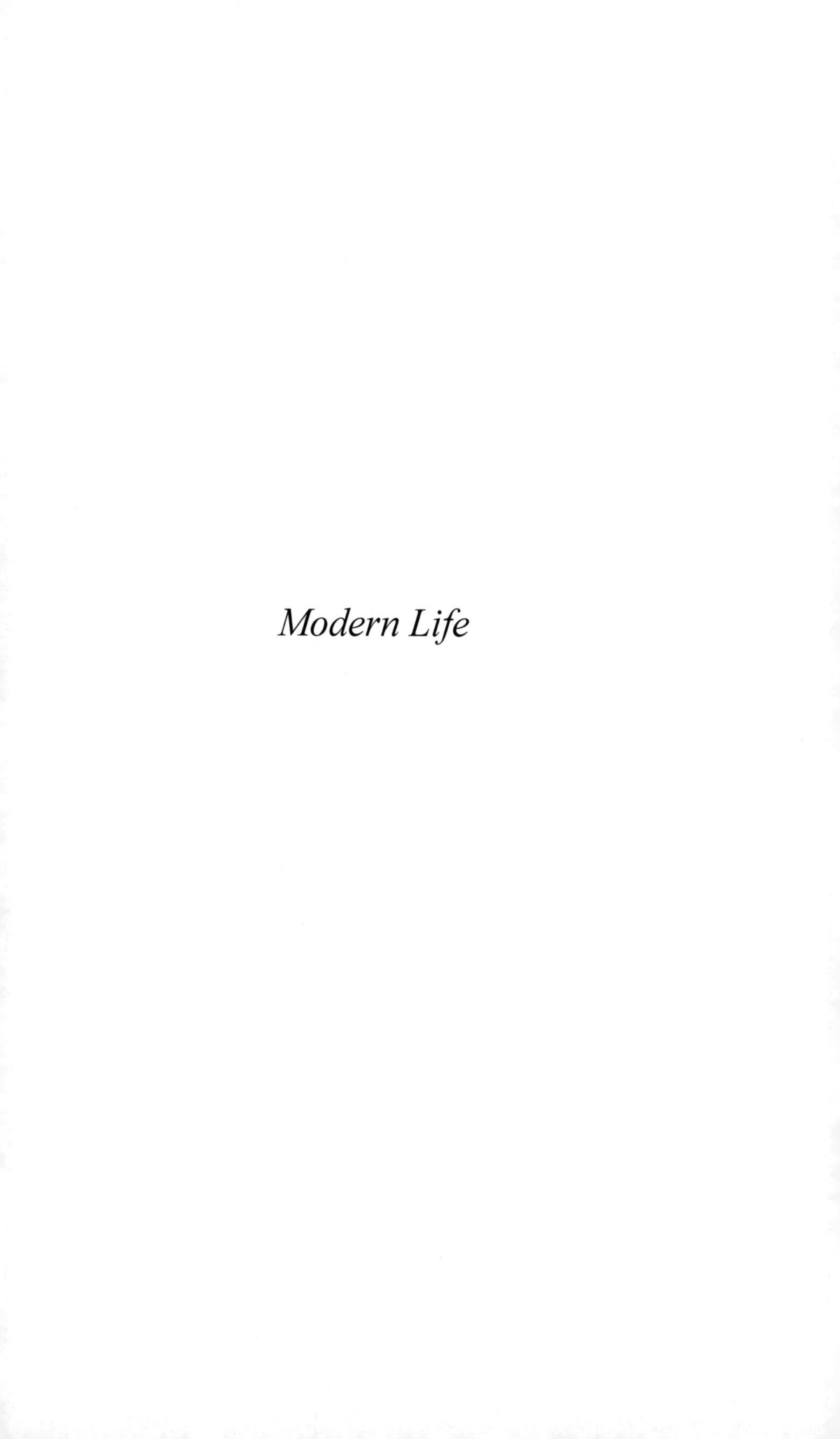

Modern Life

“The More Things Change . . .”

Outwardly the campus itself, shimmering under a Texas sun, had changed little in the ten years since she had been an undergraduate, but the dress of the students was dramatically different. Gone were the matching sweaters and skirts, the loafers and bobby sox for the women, the nicely pressed slacks and sport shirts for the men. Now women often wore jeans, just like the men. All pants had been forbidden for women on campus a decade ago.

Elizabeth was amazed by the variety of attire now, particularly among the women. One cute young undergraduate with the absolute slimness of youth climbed up the steps by the Littlefield fountain in front of her, a daring rip in her worn and faded jeans revealing the under curve of one buttock. So startlingly different, Elizabeth thought, remembering how she had been scolded as a freshman and lectured on the lasciviousness of pants. She had been waiting in the deserted parlor near the front door of the university-approved boarding house, waiting for her ride to the weekend retreat at a dude ranch, the retreat sponsored by a university social organization. The house mother had discovered her in the parlor, wearing a nice pair of tweed slacks, and had spoken to her sternly on the provocative and revealing nature of pants, the lecture so graphic she had blushed.

The south mall, though, from the Littlefield Fountain to the Main Building towering above campus, had not changed. Single students lay on the grass in the shade of live oaks, intent on their books, while small groups idled in the sunshine chatting. Parlin Hall looked the same, too. She entered the white limestone building, walked down the hall and glanced into a deserted classroom. For a moment, she could see her favorite English teacher, in suit and tie, formally ending the class before immediately lighting up a cigarette, a few earnest students gathered around him, continuing the conversation. She doubted that anyone lit up a cigarette in a classroom today.

Her interview with the creative writing professor in his second-floor office was uneventful. A boyishly attractive man in his thirties, casually yet elegantly dressed in slacks and knit shirt, Dr. Doherty merely laid out the ground rules for the independent course.

"At the end of the semester, based on the quality of the work you have produced, I will decide whether or not you are accepted into the creative writing master's program. This is independent of your course grade. You will receive three hours' credit for your work even if you are not accepted into the program, credit that will be applied to a regular master's in English."

That seemed straightforward enough.

Remembering the full professors of her undergraduate days, Elizabeth was surprised by this man's youth. His bio listed a novel he had written. Clearly he must be a rising star. Elizabeth headed to the library to check out his book.

As the semester wore on, Elizabeth turned in the first of her short stories. Professor Doherty made a few notations suggesting a syntactical change here and there, and in one place indicated that a passage should be expanded. At the end he wrote: "You write well." Nothing more.

As she sat down on the other side of the desk for the brief meeting, he leaned back in his chair, long legs elegantly stretched before him. His dark gray slacks, gray sweater over a collared maroon shirt were collegiate. He was polite, but remote. There was very little he had to say, though he went over the notations he had made on the story with her. When she got to the library, Elizabeth went over her story yet again:

WORKING TITLE: GERTIE

A gentle rain was falling outside in the late afternoon, softening the yellow-brown leaves and pressing them into the earth. Gertie was in Karen's room, listening to a Vivaldi record. Karen's parents had just given her the record player and so far the Vivaldi was the only record she owned, but it suited the afternoon and their mood, or their mood was a response to the afternoon and the record.

"What made you decide to come, after all?" Karen was asking.

How could she answer? So many memories crowded her that Gertie didn't know where to begin. Then she reordered them around the question.

"I told you about Mark, the doctor I was having an affair with in Houston. He kept telling me I ought to go to school."

Gertie remembered Mark patting her on her naked fanny, saying, "Gertie, you can't empty bedpans the rest of your life. Give it a try. Besides, I'll be there. Come to Austin, too." She owed a lot to Mark.

"Did your parents have your children then?"

"Yes. I was frantic when I found out I was pregnant again. Afterwards I was a good mother. I fed them, took care of them, but I didn't *feel* anything. My mother saw that. So she took them and I got a job as a nurse's aide in a Houston hospital."

"And that's where you met Mark?"

Gertie nodded. The cold antiseptic smell, the austere corridors. Her own shell shocked body. Mark had reawakened her. Handsome, vital, and like many doctors, self-confident to the point of arrogance. When he was overbearing, she laughed at him. When he made a crack, she one-upped him.

Gertie's eyes began to twinkle. "Did I ever tell you about the first time with him? Desperately in a hurry, we decided to meet in one of the examining rooms. I insisted it would take me ten minutes to get there, but I wouldn't explain why, though Mark didn't like it. My underwear was in tatters." Gertie began to laugh. "So I ran a block and a half to the drugstore, which had nothing but elastic girdle panties, bought a pair and cut the hose fasteners off with fingernail scissors, quick-changed in the restroom, and ran panting back to the examining room. He could hardly get them off me."

Karen laughed. She liked to hear Gertie's stories. But then she always listened to everyone. It had taken Gertie a long time to realize that although Karen talked a lot, she never confided anything. On the other hand, if you told Karen something it stayed put, an important consideration even if you were older than the bobby-soxed coeds. The rigid rules applied to all women.

Gertie's roommate, Mary Sue, square and stolid, walked in. There was an awkward pause, but Gertie slid easily over it.

"Y'all want to go get a hamburger? I've got to eat, then go to the library."

Karen had a date and declined, but Mary Sue jumped at the suggestion. Gertie had mixed feelings about Mary Sue, who had also grown up on a farm. With only a small part of her mind, Gertie could easily chat with Mary Sue, but now, as they walked down the wet sidewalk, Gertie tall, Mary Sue short and stocky, Gertie felt as though she were dragging along the weight of her own past.

When they came to the footbridge over the creek, they paused to look at the stream, running full from all the rain. The banks were dark with sodden leaves, but the creek bed was cut out of solid limestone and gleamed a little in the fading light. A wet grapevine trailed in the water just before the stream curved out of sight. Gertie could never explain to herself the attraction this spot had for her. Instead, she thought of how she would have loved to explore the creek had she been a child, then of how her children would love to play there now. For a moment, she could see Sherry squatting at the water's edge, little blond head bent over, intent, tracing the course of a water bug; in the distance, the stocky figure of her son about to disappear around the bend.

"Well, are we going to stand here all day?" Mary Sue asked, joking but still a little impatient.

Gertie jumped, then recovered herself, and walked on.

At the edge of campus they stood among the crowd of students waiting for the light to change, the women wearing skirts, often with matching blouses, most of the men in casual slacks. Almost all wore loafers, for students walked everywhere and the campus was large. In the stream of traffic, an occasional big new Buick or large-finned Chevrolet took its place among the older cars.

Across the street a line of businesses catered to students, including a corner drugstore a few blocks up that offered burgers and malts. It was about half full when they entered. Gertie spotted a German student who was in one of her classes. She had been thinking lately that he would soon make a move. Unconsciously, she brightened a little and became slightly more animated. During introductions,

Herman acknowledged Mary Sue, but since she was not attractive to him, he didn't feel he need concern himself any further than with the immediate furniture.

"Would you like to go out for a drink this evening?" Herman asked Gertie, in a slightly stilted accent, ignoring Mary Sue.

"I would love to, but I can't tonight."

Gertie knew better than to say she had to study, for she was attracted to Herman and curious. If she said she had to study, most men would take it as a subtle way of saying she didn't want to go out at all. So she let Herman think she had a prior engagement, something any man could understand.

"How about tomorrow night?"

Now that he had come this far, he was determined to press it to a conclusion. He thought Gertie wanted to go out with him, but as a foreign student he had run into an invisible barrier before.

"All right."

"Who was that?" Mary Sue asked as soon as Herman had left. She didn't consciously resent Herman's discounting her, for she was used to that by now. Men paid attention to some women and not to others. But she found Herman's accent, his very foreignness, slightly scandalous.

The evening was fresh, the air cleansed by the previous day's rain, the earth still moist and springy, as Gertie and Herman walked to his apartment. Herman moved with the abruptness of a strong, robust body, as though he had just stepped from a cold shower. As they descended the two steps to his basement apartment, he took her arm to assist her, which amused Gertie, though she could not have explained why. He ushered her into his apartment, as careful of her as though she were an egg.

The apartment consisted of a single square room which served as study, living room, and bedroom; a tiny kitchenette; and a small bathroom. Against one wall of the main room a mattress on the floor, covered with a blue spread, served both as couch and bed. Above it hung a brightly colored rug, all reds and oranges. The usual student brick and board bookshelves occupied the lower part of two other walls, a record player on top of a big record box, the fourth. In the very center of the room sat a low improvised coffee table made of concrete blocks and unpainted boards. A small candle had dripped red wax onto the center board.

Herman carefully helped her out of her sweater, then excused himself and retreated to the little kitchen for beer.

Examining the travel posters that decorated one wall—Venice, Florence, Rome—Gertie was suddenly filled with a sense of myriad unknown worlds.

“What would you like to hear?” Herman asked, returning with the beer. He was not much taller than she was, though she was a tall woman, and his eyes were brown and serious.

“I don’t know, you choose something.” Gertie liked music, listened to Karen’s battered FM radio whenever she was invited, but knew little about music. Her parents had never had a record player, though they listened to the local radio station, and much later on watched TV.

Herman put on Handel’s Water Music, then sat by her on the couch. They were both a little awkward at first, but began to relax after the first beer. After the second, Gertie offered to help him in the kitchen, but Herman refused.

Herman lit the candle on the table, one on a book shelf, and another on the record box. He turned off the lamp and put on Bach's Cantata No. 208—Sheep May Safely Graze.

Gertie was surprised when he brought out a bottle of wine to go with the spaghetti. She had never had wine with a meal before, and she had to laugh when he said, "To you, Gertie," as he raised his glass. He smiled a little at himself then, too, which made it all right. He had been so earnest about the evening.

Gertie ate heartily, which pleased Herman. They had exchanged information about themselves before, but Herman asked her to tell him some more about herself, how she came to the university.

"I don't know, my parents are just an ordinary farm family. I never thought about it until I went to Houston." She was thinking about her life with her high school boyfriend, Gary, their brief marriage after she became pregnant, remembering what it was like to clean house and care for the baby all day, fix supper for Gary, wait on him and the baby at the same time, knowing that was all she had to look forward to the next day.

Herman poured her some more wine. Their eyes met and they both smiled. Herman put another record on the turntable, then sat next to Gertie on the couch.

As the Sibelius symphony began, Gertie momentarily thought of Mark. Because he was married, she had never seen his home, but what she had seen of his life was conventional and ordinary. He had money, power, education, striking to a girl right off a modest family farm, whose parents were kind-hearted but held a suffocatingly narrow view of the world. Mark had opened Gertie's eyes. The sterile and cold corridors of the Houston hospital promised a life undreamed of by Gertie as she gently gathered eggs from henhouse nests, her bare feet squelching through yellow chicken manure. But nothing in Mark's life was like this.

The strange wild music stirred an unnamed longing in Gertie. Its dark vitality touched a responsive force deep within her and for a moment she was carried into another world.

Herman put his arm around her.

"I'm glad you left the farm."

His words jarred her, but then she began to wonder about him—the wine and candles, the strange music still pulling at her. And as he half-turned toward her, touching her cheek and kissing her, Gertie responded. Soon they leaned back until they were lying on the couch-bed, waves of music rolling over them. She had not planned on this and was not prepared, but a distant part of her mind made a quick calculation and assured her she was due to menstruate in two or three days, so she let herself go. He was fairly sure in his movements and though he came a little fast, he and the music carried her to climax.

"Thank you," he said, as they lay in the sudden stillness.

"I should thank you," Gertie answered. "It was a lovely evening."

Herman tucked her arm into his as he walked her to the front door of her rooming house. He held her hand in his and gently pressed it as he wished her good-night, but did not attempt to kiss her in the semi-public shadows of the front door.

The spartan room seemed strange, unfamiliar, as though she had never entered it before. Mary Sue was already in bed asleep, a compact lump huddled under the covers. Gertie felt disoriented, as though she had fallen down the rabbit hole, and nothing was as it had seemed all the previous years of her life. Houston, the possibility of a nursing career, fired her ambition, but though a large vision for a sheltered farm girl of the late 1950s, not impossible for her to imagine.

Gertie sat down on her bed and stared at the bare wall opposite. She saw vividly the gondola of Herman's travel poster, the gondolier poling it down a Venetian canal that gently lapped against the sides of strange buildings. Next to it, imprinted in her imagination, the Roman Colosseum, suggesting ancient and modern worlds clashing together. Worlds which her dry history texts and rote memorization of dates had made seem unreal, not exotic places where people lived and loved by different rules, according to different customs.

As the semester wore on, Gertie found herself studying more, yet feeling less certain about a nursing career. She wanted to go on an archeological dig, take an art appreciation class, study music. She worried about money, and the more her life expanded, the guiltier she felt about leaving her children. She knew she needed to take the quickest route to a career. She was rapidly depleting her savings.

Sometimes she thought of Herman. That evening had awakened old longings. Sometimes she felt the same way in her literature class, or when Karen had the stereo turned up loud. As a child on the farm, staring up at stars filling the dark summer sky, the same feelings had stirred her.

But it was not Herman. It was the music and the travel posters and the sense of unexplored worlds.

Lately, Gertie had begun dating an engineering student. Jerry was a senior, tall and lean. He worked very hard all week long, then partied on weekends. Gertie felt very comfortable with Jerry and his friends. They were much like the boys she had gone to high school with, only older and quite serious about their work and the jobs their studies would lead to. Jerry was what her parents would have called steady, and he was basically kind.

Gertie was still seeing Mark, too. Whenever he got free, he called and they would meet for whatever length of time he could get away. It always lifted her spirits to be with Mark, to see the quick warm smile come across his square open face, to feel the assurance of his big athlete's body, though sometimes the fight against time harassed her. Still, Mark would recount funny stories from the medical world, they would tease and laugh and make love—and Mark was a skilled lover, even in the back seat of a car. Mark represented a kind of security for Gertie, a safe haven where she could relax and be herself.

As much as she could, she avoided Herman. After biology class one Friday, he cut her off as she was exiting the classroom.

"There's a new German film at the Varsity that has been getting good reviews. Would you like to accompany me tonight?"

"I'm sorry, I already have plans for this evening."

Gertie did have a date with Jerry, and she was also hoping that Mark could get away to see her the next day, so when Herman suggested Saturday for the outing, she declined that offer also.

Afterwards, Herman sulked a little and left her alone for a long while. Then one day after class they had coffee together, but Gertie let him know she was going home for the weekend right away, so it was just a friendly visit.

The Sunday Gertie returned from home, Mary Sue was simply sitting in the room, staring out the window. Sometimes Gertie felt she couldn't stand that vacant look any longer, but she bustled in cheerily, anyway, for which she was glad. Mary Sue seemed so grateful Gertie had brought back dozens of eggs from the farm that Gertie suggested they fix an omelet. Karen chipped in some beer and they ate in her room. Karen, after all, had music, and Gertie could never hear enough.

"How was your trip home?"

"Oh, fine." Gertie knew that she could never explain to Karen, for it was clear that Karen had no understanding of what it meant to have a baby, to bear the responsibility for a child, to feel the conflicting claims of self and children.

"I went home Saturday, too," said Karen, whose home was just an hour's drive away. "Lots of relatives came in."

"Did you have a good visit?" Gertie was polite, but she was thinking of her own visit home. *She* was a relative, an aunt perhaps, come to visit her own children. She hardly knew her daughter. "Grandma, Grandma," Sherry cried when she was in need, a cry that cut through Gertie, though Sherry did run to embrace her mother when Gertie first arrived. With her son, who was nearly five, it was different. Sometimes, it seemed to Gertie, a look of understanding passed between them, and it was at those times that she could not bear to leave him and Sherry with her parents. One day Gertie heard her mother correcting Sherry: “No, no, Sherry, color within the lines.” The refrain haunted Gertie, Stay within the lines, within the lines. Was Sherry to be forced to stay within the lines until she stepped over the line, as Gertie had done? Sherry was a pretty child, full of life, and the vulnerability of the soft rounded contours of her face tore at Gertie.

“Yeah, I guess,” Karen said, startling Gertie out of her reverie. Karen had her own conflicts, but they were different from Gertie’s.

“I can’t wait till I can go home,” Mary Sue volunteered,

Gertie often wondered why Mary Sue ever left home in the first place. When she thought of her son and daughter growing up like that, Gertie felt desperate.

Karen was going to a movie with friends and Gertie had a date with Jerry. Mary Sue offered to clean up and free the other two to get ready. She liked to feel useful.

Gertie paused before the mirror. Actually, she wasn’t pretty, though she was pleasant looking, nor was her figure striking. She was tall, large-boned, but not particularly strong, neither thin nor heavy. Yet she knew she was attractive to men and always had been, though she didn't know why. She simply accepted it as she had accepted the other facts of her life.

Jerry was glad to see her and put his arm around her affectionately and possessively as they walked to the car.

"How was it?" he asked, with some understanding. Jerry assumed that any mother would miss her children and he had given the matter considerable thought.

"All right," Gertie said, and Jerry gave her a little squeeze.

Several couples filled the apartment on the top floor of the old house turned into student apartments: Jerry's roommates and their dates, a few other couples. The walls of the living room were mostly bare, though a dart board was fastened to one, and the furniture looked scavenged from a load headed for the dump, though the worn beige couch and mismatched, once-white overstuffed armchair were comfortable. The bare wooden floor was reasonably clean, and the room was tidy. A typical student apartment of the fifties, though better kept than many.

Three of the women were popping corn in the kitchen, standing around on the worn linoleum and chatting, talking not of their own lives, but of the men in the next room whose lives they wanted to share. As Gertie and Jerry entered the apartment, the women brought in the popcorn and momentarily joined the men laughing and talking in the living room, relaxed with their beers now that the work week had ended.

Gertie felt vaguely oppressed and discontented, but she greeted everyone merrily and the feeling slipped away.

As Jerry was taking her home, he suddenly said, “Why don’t you bring your son up for the weekend sometime so I can get to know him. You could sign out as though you were going home for the weekend, but both stay here.”

Gertie was surprised and moved. “Are you sure you want to do that?”

“Yes, I am,” Jerry said firmly.

A few weeks later, Gertie brought her son up and stayed at the apartment with Jerry. While she cooked supper, Jerry and Todd went outside to toss a football back and forth. Gertie could see them from the kitchen window, which looked out over the small back yard. Tall and lean, precise in his movements, Gertie could easily see Jerry as the solid high school athlete he had once been.

Jerry kidded Todd, rough-housed with him and was quietly affectionate. Todd pushed to see how far he could go, but Jerry was firm and Todd quit being wild. By the end of the weekend, Todd idolized Jerry.

"I know how you feel," Jerry said to Gertie. "I know you want to get them off the farm. I love my parents, too, but I realized a long time ago that there wasn't any money in farming. A man has to get a good job if he's going to provide a good life for his family."

Gertie didn't say anything.

The next time Gertie saw Herman, she was with Jerry. He had her by the waist and was guiding her into the movie. Herman looked a little wistful, but there seemed no need to say anything.

Karen was surprised when Gertie told her that she and Jerry planned to marry, but she didn't say anything and Gertie didn't try to explain. Karen was even more surprised when Gertie told her that Jerry didn't want to make love any more until after they were married.

"But why?" Karen asked. She really meant, why are *you* marrying a man like that?

"Oh, I don't know, he's just like that." Gertie thought about the first time she and Jerry made love. He was a little awkward, which checked Gertie a bit, and then he came so fast that Gertie had no chance at all. Fortunately, Gertie was an experienced woman and helped Jerry along. When she spent the night at his apartment, they often made love two or three times in the course of the night, which gave them a chance to work things out.

"I don't know," Gertie said, though she had made up her mind. When she had told him, Mark saw no reason why her marriage should affect their relationship. He thought it a good thing. He had a daughter whom he loved dearly, and he was glad Gertie could provide a home for her children. "I can't do it, Mark," she said. "That wouldn't be fair to Jerry." Gertie had sometimes enjoyed the sense of secrecy in her relationship with Mark, as though they shared something exciting that no one else knew about, but this was clearly different. She would be vowing sexual fidelity to Jerry.

"But you don't believe in that," Mark said.

"I know, but Jerry does. I can't enter the marriage with that kind of secret." Mark was disappointed, but he didn't press her. It was difficult enough for Gertie. Her life looked bleaker.

Wisteria bloomed, left lavender drifts on sidewalks, dusted car hoods with pastel purple. Spring deepened, and Gertie threw herself into details. She registered Todd for kindergarten, found a nursery school for Sherry that wasn't too expensive. She and Jerry planned to marry at the end of the school year. That would give the four of them the summer to become a family before the fall semester. Jerry had an assistantship for the next year and a good job for the summer, good enough to help them through the school year. Gertie was to stay at home with the children during the summer to ease them through the transition.

As she had done growing up on the farm, Gertie arose early every morning, so that Jerry could emerge from his shower to a hot breakfast: steaming coffee, bacon and eggs and toast; sometimes the children's favorite, pancakes and sausage. Then, a cheerful kiss for Gertie and one for Sherry, a rumpling of Todd's hair, and Jerry was off to work for the day. Efficient and well organized, Gertie quickly had the apartment to rights.

She had given much thought to the education of her children. She walked them all over the campus, letting them play in the little creek in the remoter part of campus some days. Other days they wandered among the statues and fountains. Sherry particularly loved the raring horses with the fountain, sparkling in the sunlight, playing over them. Todd was drawn to Civil War heroes, erect on their splendid horses, swords buckled at their sides. Some days they walked to the local library and returned with a stack of books for Gertie to read to the children in the long hot afternoons, with always a couple for her. Like most housing of the time, their apartment had no air conditioning, and when the children grew restless in the stifling heat, Gertie would walk them to the deeply shaded park not too far away. While they played on the swings and seesaws and climbed on the jungle gym with the few other children in the little park, Gertie would read, sometimes a novel suggested by an English class, sometimes an archeology text, occasionally glancing up to check on the children.

By July, the summer seemed endless. Although they were excited by all the new adventures, the children missed the farm and their grandparents. Sherry in particular missed her grandmother and sometimes had crying fits. Todd occasionally pushed the boundaries hard, generally when he was over tired. But Jerry was a good father. Sherry adored him. He spent a little time with them each evening when he got off work, and on weekends the four of them went on picnics, had friends over for supper. Jerry liked to see Gertie in the little kitchen of their apartment preparing supper. He often played with the kids to keep them off her hands while she cooked.

Sometimes, when Sherry was crying and hanging onto her leg, while Jerry was in the backyard tossing a football to Todd, and she was trying to put a casserole in the hot oven, and the sweat was pouring down her face in the stifling kitchen, and Sherry wouldn't stop crying . . . Gertie would tell herself that in the fall her own life would begin again.

Autumn finally came, and with it the excitement of classes. But it was harder than Gertie had anticipated, a struggle to get the children off in the morning: a misplaced tennis shoe, a fight over which pretty top to wear (the favorite being in the dirty clothes), a last-minute tantrum. There was laundry to do for four people, groceries to buy, the apartment to clean. In the evenings the children came back tired and hungry, overstimulated from their day. By the time Gertie finished with the supper dishes and got the children to bed, she was exhausted. And sometimes at night Sherry had nightmares.

Finally, Gertie had to drop two courses.

"Don't worry, honey," Jerry said. "You don't need a degree. Soon I'll have a really good job. You won't ever have to do anything."

Gertie couldn't explain the sudden chill she felt.

She finally finished the semester with nine hours credit. She decided to try taking twelve in the spring. The children had settled into their routines better and Gertie thought she could manage it.

"Don't kill yourself, Gertie," Jerry said. "What's the point in it? Besides, as soon as I get a job, we could afford to have a baby."

Gertie began to panic. She didn't want another child. She and Jerry had not discussed having children before they married, but now Jerry was assuming that she would want to have his child. In fact, it never crossed his mind that they would not eventually have a child of their own.

Gertie noticed that Jerry had become careless about contraception. Before, he had always asked her if she were wearing her diaphragm first, but once or twice lately he had been insistent even when she wasn't prepared. It ruined it for Gertie. She had started putting on the diaphragm whenever she thought there was a possibility she might need it. And, too, she was so exhausted by bedtime these days that she was losing interest in sex.

One Sunday afternoon while the children were asleep and Jerry was at the library, she sat by herself, staring listlessly out the window. The sky was overcast, with an intermittent drizzle. The crooked limbs of a live oak, turned black by the rain, were silhouetted against the gray sky.

Her books were piled haphazardly at the end of the couch, but she didn't have the energy to pick one up. Dirty dishes were stacked in the sink, forgotten. A few toys and children's books were scattered on the rug. Soon she would need to start supper, but she couldn't rouse herself. She felt imprisoned.

The rain started up in earnest, splattering against the windowpanes. The live oak turned hazy in the downpour, and the sky darkened.

The more she reflected on her life, the less she was able to see any solution. Her parents, though they missed the children, her mother in particular, were thrilled that she now had a stable home and a good husband able to provide for them all. What more could a woman want? A kind man who had taken on her two children, who was a good father to them and soon would be able to give the family a very comfortable life. Of course he would want a child of his own, too. She was very lucky.

Gertie despaired.

The hard rain had slackened, now falling slowly under the darkened sky, slowly dripping down the streaked windowpanes and falling gently onto the sodden earth.

I need to talk to someone, she said to herself, desperately. She looked at the books piled on the couch, at the toys on the floor, turned to gaze out at the wet grey desolate world. Who would understand?

Suddenly she thought of Mark. For a moment she felt a surge of her old vitality as she picked up the phone, and also some trepidation. She had never called him at his home before. Fortunately, he was the one who answered.

"Mark," she said, "I've changed my mind. Let me know whenever you have a few hours free."

"Wonderful," he said.

When she left the library, Elizabeth was still thinking about the story, based on one of the students she had known in the small rooming house her junior year. Night had fallen while she was in the library, but this part of the campus was well lighted and many students were about. She was generally alert to her surroundings when she needed to be.

She carried Dr. Doherty's novel with her. She was curious about him and always interested in new writers.

On the way back to her friend's apartment, which was less than a mile from campus, she passed small eateries and a few crowded bars before reaching the less well lighted residential streets. A crescent moon was visible through the crooked branches of occasional live oaks in this older neighborhood. She passed columned, two-storey fraternity houses; large older homes, slightly dilapidated, that had been divided up into student housing; an occasional duplex; modest single-family homes still inhabited by long-time residents. A few students traveled the streets or chatted together on a front porch, drinking a beer. Three students walking briskly stepped off the sidewalk in order to pass around her. The young woman was in front, looking straight ahead and ignoring the two men's comments. Elizabeth stopped suddenly and glared at the men, the authority of a mother in her face. One of the men, looking back at Elizabeth, tried to restrain his friend and gave Elizabeth an apologetic look. The other paused only briefly, then resumed his harassing. All three were shortly out of sight.

"Why didn't I say something," Elizabeth scolded herself. At least there were people about, so no real physical danger. She remembered vividly one night when she had been an undergraduate, 21 and a senior, and therefore finally free to have her own apartment, free of university oversight. About ten o'clock she had run out of paper as she typed up a report due the next day on her well worn portable typewriter. Her apartment above an unused detached garage was less than half a mile from the nearest office supplies store on the Drag, so she started out on foot, her only means of transportation, as was true for the majority of students back then. She was astounded by the catcalls and rude comments that followed her the whole way, and even a whiff of danger as a car full of young men pulled alongside her, following at her pace. She was furious and unbelieving. This was the university area. It dawned on

her that she had never been out alone at night in the city before and had therefore never confronted the underlying reality.

Now she walked on, dissatisfied with herself for not having challenged the harassing young men, but still happily anticipating a quiet evening with her friend. It was a relief to have this one night away from her husband and children, to know she could get some work done without interruptions.

~ ~ ~

It was such a common occurrence back then, Elizabeth thought, four decades later, yet we didn't have the tools for challenging the men. She thought about the next story she had written so many years ago. The themes for her stories had come to her, but she still hadn't had the full conceptual framework for addressing those issues.

She remembered that young professor Doherty had had even less to say about the next story she had submitted to him. She drew the yellowed manuscript from the stack of old papers she had found going through dusty ancient boxes. It was still labelled with the working title, a manuscript written on an old manual typewriter and frayed a little at the edges.

Working title: **Mary Sue**

The western sun streamed through the front window of the living room, making patterns on the flowered blue linoleum. The ticking of the clock on the corner whatnot shelf was the only sound in the afternoon quiet. Some of the figurines on the two shelves below the clock were lighted up by the late afternoon sun: the gold trim of the little shepherdess, the plump outlines of the salt and pepper cherubs; the glossy black panther ivy holder—without ivy—on the shelf below. In a little while, the afternoon chores would begin, but now all was calm and peaceful.

Mary Sue was thinking of this as she joked with her parents and prepared to say goodbye.

“Have you got everything, now?” her mother said. “We don’t want to forget anything.” Fussing about details was her way of showing concern for her family; everything had been carefully packed and gone over hours ago.

Mary Sue nodded, her throat tightening. She was a squarely-built, stolid girl and her face didn’t show the sudden panic she felt.

“We best be getting on back,” her father said at the stop, as Mary Sue stared at the steps up into the bus. He, too, was short and stocky, with a round head, a round weathered face, and widely separated teeth, which gave him a buffoonish air, particularly when he was ill at ease.

“Study hard, now,” he said, giving Mary Sue a clumsy half-hug, his voice slightly breaking on the last word.

Mary Sue watched out the window of the Greyhound bus until the old Chevrolet disappeared around the corner. Then she pulled her knitting out of her large pocketbook.

The fields rolled past, most of the corn already harvested, the cotton still standing, the heavy bolls white with unpicked cotton.

When they finally reached it, the city of two hundred thousand seemed enormous to her. There was too much to see, and it exhausted her. She had never before paid a taxi driver and she very carefully counted out the money, making sure she got it right.

The boarding house seemed comfortable enough, not as orderly as her own home, but comfortable. The parlor, with its best furniture, didn't seem much used, but then parlors rarely were. Mrs. Armstrong seemed nice and showed her the outside stairs that led to the second floor where the four student rooms were.

She climbed the stairs, walked through the kitchenette and into her own room, wondering who her roommate would be. No one else was around this time of day.

She was pleased about the kitchenette. Not only would it save money, but Mary Sue was glad she could fix her own meals. For a moment she toyed with the idea of cooking something, but gave it up. She sat down by the window, folded her hands in her lap. Something about the way she sat, the unusual feeling of the day, brought back memories, warm secure memories she could hold on to.

It was Sunday afternoon and two of her aunts, her mother's sisters, were visiting. Her father had excused himself as soon as he decently could and had taken her younger brother with him, leaving the women to themselves. Mary Sue sat very properly on the couch beside her mother, her hands folded in her lap. Across the room, on the other side of the little round table with the candy box centered on the doily, sat the aunts. The candy box had always fascinated Mary Sue, not only because it had sweets in it, but because of the two elves with their green pointed boots and green pointed caps, leaning back to back to form the handle of the lid.

"Why, I declare. Did you do that all by yourself, Mary Sue?" Her aunt was examining the pillow case Mary Sue had embroidered.

"Yes'm."

"Well, maybe with just a little bit of help—but not much," her mother said, unable to conceal her pride.

"That's real good for a little girl your age, Mary Sue," her other aunt said, putting on her glasses to look at the pillow case more closely.

Mary Sue's reverie was suddenly interrupted by the entrance of her roommate. Gertie was a tall, fairly large woman, pleasant-faced, and Mary Sue was reassured to find out that Gertie, too, had grown up on a farm. Gertie, however, was a good bit older. She had married at the end of her senior year in high school, had had a baby shortly thereafter, then another. She had divorced her husband, worked as a nurse's aide in a city hospital, and then, at age twenty-three, decided to go to college. Her parents were raising her children and giving her a little money.

Mary Sue didn't learn all this at once, but enough to make her wonder about her new roommate. But Gertie was down to earth, quite open about her history, and easy to get along with.

"Why don't we put one desk here and the other one over there?" Mary Sue suggested. She was relieved to have the details of arranging the room to attend to, and glad that Gertie had come in so they could organize things.

"Okay." Fortunately, Gertie had no fixed ideas about where the furniture ought to go.

Several weeks later, Mary Sue lay in her bed, listening to the unfamiliar city noises. She was trying to order all the unaccustomed experiences of the last few weeks. She was pretty good on directions, and by now had an accurate mental map of the campus, though it still seemed strange to her. The live oaks, the limestone buildings reflecting the light, the civil war statues and fountains, all seemed exotic to her. And so many people, young people, all self-confident, so sure of where they were going.

But most bewildering were her classes. It had been easy at home. The teacher made it clear what she wanted, and if you did your lessons carefully, you satisfied her. And if you still didn't understand, you could always go up to the teacher and ask her. In fact, it was sometimes helpful to do that even when you did understand, so that she would know you were trying. But here, Mary Sue couldn't figure out what it was that her professors wanted. Her home economics course was the only place she felt at home.

Once she had accidentally missed a class and had been quite apprehensive when she went to it the next time. Nobody cared, or even knew whether she had been there or not. The sudden realization that she could do whatever she wanted and nobody would know or care frightened her.

The light from the streetlamp outside bothered her. At home, after she was in bed, the only light came from the moon and stars and it was quite dark in her room. You could touch yourself in the night, and the dark was dense and secret. Her thighs spread a little and waves of unfocused desire swept her. She remembered the gossip her best friend used to tell her.

"Did you hear about Betty and Don?"

"No, what?"

"They got caught doing it behind the curtains at the back of the auditorium."

"No!"

"Yes! Standing up."

The scandal had been all over the school in an afternoon, though the administration tried to keep it quiet. And there were secret whisperings about other couples, who had done it and how far someone else had gone. Mary Sue was intensely titillated, but she could not understand how anyone could survive the shame of being discovered, of having everyone know that you had Done It.

She turned away from the window toward the darkened room and drifted toward sleep.

In high school, Mary Sue had not dated, though she found many of the boys attractive. She was on easy terms with almost everyone, but no one asked her out. Her father was rather glad, but her mother thought it was time she found some steady young man.

"But since it don't look like she's going to get married, she best do something. Times are changing," her father said.

"And maybe she'll meet someone off at college," mused her mother, thinking of how Miss Jones had praised Mary Sue. "No reason she can't be married and a home economics teacher, too. For a little while, anyway."

Mary Sue was the first in her family to go to college.

The next morning, Mary Sue rose early, with the first light, and bustled about, dressing, making her bed, cooking breakfast and cleaning up afterward. Then she had nothing to do. She didn't have a class until ten, and it was only eight. Everyone else was asleep. She thought about studying, but didn't know where to start. Finally, she picked up her algebra book and sat at her desk. She had always been pretty good in math, but here she had gotten behind. Her professor left so much up to them that Mary Sue found herself doing nothing.

She thought about Gertie, wondered what she did on all those dates. Here Gertie had been married and had two children, you know she didn't just hold hands on dates. She tried to picture what it would be like on the back seat of some car.

Karen stumbled out of her room and began to make coffee. Mary Sue came to the door.

"Good morning."

"Morning," Karen mumbled. She had little to say before she had had a couple of cups of coffee, though then she could be talkative enough.

Karen was lithe and pretty, though disheveled now. Mary Sue was puzzled by her. She wasn't stuck-up; she went out of her way to talk to everyone. But she had a room to herself, even though she had to pay double for it, and often shut herself up alone. When she wasn't studying, she was partying, and often kept a six-pack of beer in the refrigerator in flagrant violation of the rules. She reminded Mary Sue a little of the wild and pretty high school girls, yet whatever they did was covert, was whispered of them behind their backs. But Karen spoke openly of free love, claiming she could see nothing wrong in it as long as you were responsible about contraception. Yet Mary Sue could not tell that Karen practiced what she preached. Although she partied a lot and chafed about rules and regulations, about the hours they all had to keep, it seemed to Mary Sue that the boys Karen knew were just friends.

Mary Sue's stomach knotted and then she began to ache with desire as she thought of what *she* would do if *she* believed there was no wrong in it. But her plain, expressionless face showed nothing.

Karen hurried off to class, late, after her second cup of coffee, and Mary Sue checked the time once more. Still almost an hour before her class, not that she especially wanted to go to it, but she had nothing else to do. And it was part of what little order her days had.

Mary Sue thought of home. The big clean kitchen with all its familiar tools, the early morning light and the smell of fresh coffee. Her father and brother stomping and joking around on the back porch, hacking and spitting before they came into the kitchen where she and her mother were setting out the breakfast. The day was carefully measured out and you never had to stop and think what to do.

Once more she looked at her watch and this time found that she could start to class.

That afternoon almost everyone else seemed to come back at the same time. Mary Sue had just baked a pan of brownies and was offering them around. Brownies were a favorite of her father's, and he was always pleased with her when she baked.

"Mary Sue been in the kitchen again, I see."

She could see him now coming in from the barn, a faint reek of cow manure about him. That was something else she missed, smells: turned earth and hay, cow piss and manure. She thought of the big Hereford bull, square-hipped and lumbering, grunting and sniffing and trying to mount a cow, and finally, when the cow herself was ready and would let him, a quick few thrusts and it was over. And Mary Sue ached with loneliness.

Ida had come in just before Karen and couldn't wait to tell her.

"You're in trouble with Mrs. Armstrong for spending the night out."

Ida was lean and angular, of recent German descent, and would have been attractive except for a certain gracelessness. Her room was nearest the outside door and she had appointed herself guardian of morals. Mrs. Armstrong liked to go to bed early and assumed that everyone would come in when they were supposed to—or didn't care. This was not rigorous enough for Ida and she insisted on locking the upstairs door and keeping a careful accounting of who came and went, at what hours, and reporting to Mrs. Armstrong. Ida was secretly triumphant, waiting for Karen to cringe.

"No, she called my cousin. I forgot to sign out," Karen said carelessly.

Ida was obviously disappointed and frustrated.

Mary Sue was watching, wondering to herself. Ida was clearly the most disagreeable person in the boarding house, and she was the only representative of all that Mary Sue herself had been taught. Everyone else on the floor had been forced to demand from Mrs. Armstrong an extra long telephone cord because the phone was just outside Ida's room, and Ida felt it her duty to eavesdrop on everyone's conversations. She was also stingy. Even now she was helping herself to several of Mary Sue's brownies, but if Ida ever baked, she carried it all into her room and closed the door. And everyone had begun to notice about the coffee, too. It was the custom that whenever anyone made coffee, they invited the others to have a cup, and so it balanced out. But although Ida always helped herself, she perked her coffee behind closed doors.

Mary Sue began to tidy up, her square, heavy body moving efficiently in the kitchenette. She puzzled about Ida. Instinctively she banded together with the others in common dislike of Ida, yet she had to admit that Ida was standing up for what she herself had been taught was right.

Janie came in, declined a brownie, headed for her room. She was a small, neurasthenic brunette, something of a leftist, and an elitist. Although she was unfailingly polite, her life was elsewhere, and she did not pretend an interest in her fellow roomers. Janie lived with her boyfriend on weekends, studied in her room the rest of the week, when she was there. To Mary Sue, it seemed clear that Janie thought herself too good to associate with anyone there.

"What'd she want to live here for, anyway?" she asked Gertie.

"She's got to live somewhere, and this place is cheaper than most."

"Why doesn't she just move in with her boyfriend all the time? That would be cheapest."

Gertie laughed, but it still took some time before Mary Sue realized her own witticism.

The next Sunday seemed endless to Mary Sue. She had not gone to church that morning, but had lain in bed, watching the sunlight filter through the leaves of the live oak outside her window. There were no live oaks on the farm and Mary Sue felt slightly uncomfortable around them. She could not have said why the unexpected angles of the limbs disturbed her. That's just not the way a tree is supposed to look, she would have said.

She could not seem to find a reason to get up that morning, though she knew she should dress for church. She thought of home, and the whole family getting ready. Her father in his dark suit—a striking contrast to his usual overalls. Her adolescent brother, gangling and awkward in his new suit, the cuffs already too short on his long arms.

"Now hurry up or we'll be late," her mother said, patting down the skirt of her grey dress, speaking to no one in particular, though they were all ready and had been for some time. And indeed, the family had never been known to be late to anything.

Mary Sue had made her own dress and was satisfied with the way it fit, pleased with the appearance of the whole family. They were all properly dressed, very respectable, but none of them ever wore anything flashy. Not one of her family would ever stick out like a sore thumb, she thought.

But this morning, Mary Sue could not find a reason for going to church. I don't know anyone, she thought, remembering how strange and unfamiliar church here had seemed, how awkward she had felt. And no one here knew or cared whether or not you went to church. Karen laughed at the whole idea, Gertie expressed no opinion but in fact usually slept till noon, and Janie, God knows what Janie was doing on Sunday mornings. And Mary Sue wondered what it must be like to be writhing and moaning on a rumpled bed while everyone else sat stiffly on a wooden pew, dressed in Sunday clothes.

Finally, Mary Sue had gotten up and fixed herself a big meal, but it seemed rather pointless. Cleaning up in the kitchen made her feel a little better, for that was clearly necessary work. Then she walked the few blocks to the drug store, bought some toothpaste and acne cream, drank a coke and watched people stroll by outside, mostly couples hand in hand. Then she walked back. Karen was sitting on the grass a few houses down from Mrs. Armstrong's talking with the guys who lived there. It seemed to Mary Sue that all Karen ever did was talk, except when she shut herself up to study.

Gertie had not come back and the room seemed cold and lonely when Mary Sue entered. It occurred to her that she ought to write her parents. She got out her stationary, a pen, adjusted the desk light, and tried to begin.

"Hi." Gertie swept into the room, loaded down with cartons of eggs.

"My folks had plenty of eggs," she said. "Maybe I'll make it through this month."

Mary Sue felt better at once. She was grateful to Gertie. Some of the eggs were still smeared with a little chicken shit, and Mary Sue found herself wanting to hold them in her hands, as though she had just taken them from the nest herself. She remembered when she had gotten big enough to be allowed to gather the eggs. It was like Easter every morning. And she had been very careful never to break one. For a moment her nose filled with the strong smell of the inside of the chicken house and she could feel the squish of the shit under her bare feet.

Karen came in and Gertie proposed that they all make an omelet.

"How was your visit?" Karen asked.

"Oh, fine," Gertie answered noncommittally. She had confided a lot in Karen and had jested about her own sexual adventures with a keen sense of the ludicrous, but no one here had ever had children and did not know what it was to go home occasionally to them, both missing them and feeling guilty for missing them so little. Mary Sue occasionally saw a look pass between Gertie and Karen, as though they knew something that she didn't, but she wasn't so dumb, she thought, she knew what Gertie was up to.

Mary Sue made toast while Karen found a piece of cheese for the omelet. When it was ready, Karen invited them to come into her room to eat.

"I've got some beer."

"Great," Gertie said, "I could use one."

Mary Sue hesitated for an instant. She had never had a beer before. Her father liked his beer, and she knew all the high school boys drank. She suspected that her brother had come in drunk a time or two, though no one else knew. But her mother did not drink. It was understood that high school girls did not drink, though it was whispered that an occasional one had a beer with her boyfriend. But Mary Sue was tempted, and tried to be very casual about it.

"Sure," she said, though she took the can rather awkwardly. Surprisingly, she didn't mind the taste.

After they ate, it was time for Gertie to dress for a date and Karen had planned to go to a movie with several friends. Mary Sue offered to do the cleaning up.

"Oh, thanks," Karen said.

"That would be great," Gertie said. "Jerry hates to wait."

In a moment of daring, Mary Sue suddenly said, "Doesn't Jerry have a friend who might need a date sometime?"

"I'll see," Gertie offered.

As the semester wore on, Mary Sue began to be quite cavalier about her studies. She found herself bragging about having to cram for a test the night before. She began to assimilate the party-girl attitude toward her schoolwork without leading a party-girl life. Sometimes she remembered her high school days. People clustered in the hall before a test anxiously going over their notes, or simply moaning, or proudly announcing how little they had studied or how late they had stayed up.

"Here comes Mary Sue. Bet she's not scared."

And Mary Sue would walk down the hall, stocky and plain, but smug and satisfied. *She* had not stayed up all night, but had gone to bed as usual, and *she* was prepared. It was all a matter of doing your assignments on time, every day, and keeping up. She was as methodical in her schoolwork as she was in her life. If only her professors here would tell her what to do every day. How could she do what she was supposed to do if she didn't know what it was?

A vague apprehension would grip Mary Sue and she would rush to find someone to talk to.

One evening, Mary Sue wandered into the kitchenette, wondering if it was worthwhile trying to talk to Ida. Gertie was studying for an exam, and Karen wasn't back yet.

There was an impatient rapping on the door.

"You're thirty-five minutes late," Ida said, letting Karen in.

"So what," Karen answered coldly.

"Mrs. Armstrong isn't going to like it."

"I don't imagine she gives a damn." And Karen brushed past Ida toward her own room.

"Goddamn rules," she stormed, furious with the restrictions on her freedom. "A really interesting conversation and I have to think about these goddamn rules." By this time, Karen was pacing up and down.

Ida retreated to her room and closed the door.

Mary Sue's eyes widened slightly, but otherwise she did not show the slight shock she felt, not at the tantrum so much as at the language, at the openness of it, that is. Of course, women—young women—used profanity among themselves, among friends, but with an emphasis, an understanding that it was secret and obscene. But Karen used “goddamn” as though there were nothing special about it, as though she didn’t care who heard her. And indeed, Mary Sue had once overheard her speak as freely in a group of her male friends.

“I don’t think I can stand some prurient Dean of Women telling me what to do much longer,” Karen said, but settling down a little now.

“It’s just as easy to get pregnant before midnight as after, if that’s what they’re worried about,” Gertie said.

You should know, thought Mary Sue.

Janie stuck her head out of her door and uncharacteristically joined the conversation.

“Did you know the Dean of Women’s office spends its time keeping check on everyone not in approved housing, regardless of how old the women are?”

“I’m not surprised,” Karen said.

“I have a friend who shares her apartment with a man—not her boyfriend, who doesn’t like it too much, either, but a homosexual. He sleeps on her couch and does all the housework, every bit of it. The Dean of Women called her in, but actually, she's exploiting him."

Everyone but Mary Sue, who was absolutely baffled, appreciated the irony. Mary Sue's impassive countenance didn't reveal the struggle she was having. Why would Janie's friend (and what kind of person was Janie that she had such friends?) share an apartment with a queer instead of her boyfriend? And why would she want someone else to do her own work? If I were going to have a man living in my apartment, it sure wouldn't be a queer, Mary Sue thought. And she grew hot all over, thinking about that man lying on her couch, while she lay waiting for him in the secret dark.

The following Saturday, Gertie said, "Jerry's roommate Don needs a date tonight. Want to go?"

"Sure," Mary Sue said.

When Mary Sue walked into the parlor downstairs with Gertie, there was Jerry, waiting for them. She looked at the shelves and shelves of figurines on the wall and wondered that Mrs. Armstrong had collected so many. Mrs. Armstrong's arrangements were not geometrically precise, but the variety of rosy-cheeked cherubs, gold-haired ballerinas, big-bellied gnomes, and shepherdesses with their sheep made up in interest what they lacked in careful arrangement. For a moment she was carried back to the time when as a little girl she had visited a distant relative with her mother. She had almost forgotten her manners she had been so entranced by the cousin's collection of pretty things: shells and figurines, clocks, and best of all, music boxes. She was struck by a wave of nostalgia for her childhood, for her own well-ordered home.

She was lost in thought a moment, but when Jerry said, "Well, it took y'all long enough," and Gertie turned to her and said, "I told you he'd say that," Mary Sue answered, "Well, you weren't waiting for me, *I* was ready," and plunged toward the door.

The small apartment seemed crowded. It was filled with noise and smoke. Mary Sue blinked a little when she entered.

"Where's Don?" Jerry asked, then made the introductions as Don lurched up, already half drunk.

"Glad to know you," Don said, giving Mary Sue an appraising look. He was trim and wiry, had played basketball and run track for his small-town high school. Mary Sue had gone to school with boys like him. He had a small muscled seat and carried himself lightly, though he was a little unsteady now from drink.

"Wanna dance," he said, reaching out unceremoniously for Mary Sue. She held her breath for a moment as he took her in his arms, then let herself relax and melt into him. She was a surprisingly good dancer, in spite of her ungainly appearance, and when he shut his eyes, it felt good to him.

He offered her a beer after the dance and she drank it all, which surprised him. He experimented with holding her very close and moving his pelvis into hers. She clung to him and when he moved his hand down her back to her bottom, she began to breathe hard.

In a little while, he got two more beers and led her into the back bedroom off the kitchen and closed the door. She grunted sharply when he entered her, but she never wanted him to stop, even though it took him awhile because of all the drink.

Afterward, Don rolled off and then passed out where he lay. Mary Sue was glad. She didn't know how she could walk out the door and face everybody, but it was getting close to curfew time.

She straightened her clothes one more time, took a deep breath and walked out into the kitchen, a little unsteadily. The light hurt her eyes and disoriented her.

Gus, who shared the apartment with Jerry and Don, was sitting on a stool by the kitchen counter, leaning up against it, too drunk to risk the use of his legs. He was large, easygoing, a little shapeless, and essentially benevolent. He looked up when Mary Sue opened the door, interrupting his contemplation of the kitchen linoleum.

"Try holding your legs together when you walk," Gus said helpfully.

And it seemed to Mary Sue for an instant that she had no clothes on and that Gus could see the sticky semen dripping down her leg. She rushed into the more dimly lighted living room and found Gertie and Jerry ready to go.

"Karen's a hypocrite," Mary Sue was saying to Gertie one day. "She's always saying she doesn't see anything wrong in doing it. So why isn't she out doing it?"

Gertie didn't know exactly what to say, but Mary Sue didn't want an answer. She felt she shared a guilty secret with Gertie and could only relieve herself by talking, so that she was beginning to get on Gertie's nerves.

"She almost climaxed the first time, she said, in spite of its hurting," Gertie told Karen in some amazement. She had a strong sense of the ribald and had often amused Karen with her own stories, but she withdrew from Mary Sue's agony. Her own moral struggle was quite different, and it was hard for her to take agonizing over virginity, or the lack of it, seriously.

Sometimes Gertie's casual attitude about sex relieved Mary Sue, and she often reminded herself that Janie regularly slept with her boyfriend. But when she thought about the world she had left, tried to picture how her parents would feel if they knew, what all her relatives and friends would think of her, she knew she had sinned, totally and irrevocably, and the enormity of it overwhelmed her. At such moments, she would begin to straighten up the room, reorganize her things, plan menus for the next few days. And then it would strike her that she ought to be married and doing these things in her own home for her husband. But she had not seen Don again. He had not called her or expressed any interest in seeing her again. And sometimes, when she thought of that night, she was racked with desire until she thought she would scream.

One night when she was trying to study for an exam, Gertie called her from the apartment. There was loud music and laughter in the background, and Gertie told her Don wanted to talk to her.

"Why don't you get your ass over here," he took the phone to say, his tongue a little thick.

Mary Sue flamed up with desire, but said nothing.

Gertie got back on the phone.

"Do you want Jerry to come get you?"

"I don't know, what do you think?"

"Do what you want," Gertie said casually.

"I better not, I don't know. I'll call you back."

Mary Sue went into Karen's room.

"There's a big party at Jerry's. Don wants me to come over, but I've got a big test tomorrow. Do you think I ought to go?"

Karen was very careful. "That's something you have to decide for yourself."

Mary Sue wandered out, disappointed. I've got to study, she thought, and returned to her desk. She picked up a book without noticing which one it was. A slow, dull ache ate into her.

"Tell Jerry to come get me," she said into the phone.

Everyone began to notice that Mary Sue was acting strange. Karen saw her come in from class, put on an apron and place a skillet on the stove. Then she took off her apron, sat at her desk for a moment, then came back into the kitchenette and put on the apron again. Gertie reported that some days she never seemed to leave their room, just sat silent, staring at the wall behind her desk. When Janie was staying up all night studying, she saw Mary Sue wandering around as though she didn't see where she was going. Finally Gertie talked Mrs. Armstrong into calling Mary Sue's parents to come get her. Everyone stood under the big live oak and said good-by.

Just before she stepped into the old Chevrolet, Mary Sue turned and said, "I'm going to get married," and then, "Just kidding." And she began to laugh.

Dr. Doherty had even less to say about this story. He had marked a few awkward places in the writing, indicated a passage that needed clarifying. Although again he went over the story with her in his office, he merely repeated verbally the notations in the margins. This was

Elizabeth's first—and as it turned out, only—creative writing course. She hadn't known what to expect, but Professor Doherty seemed so detached, quite noncommittal, almost dismissive. Still, Elizabeth felt pretty good about the stories themselves. Professor Doherty was clearly well organized, spent the exact amount of time allotted to the conference, nothing more, nothing less. He rose to his feet with a casual grace to let her know when the time was up, was distantly polite as she exited the office.

She remembered the English professors of her undergraduate years, much older men, classically educated and formal in their manners, deeply respected by the students. In turn, Elizabeth thought, we felt their respect and caring for us. It had been a wonderful time in her life.

Just one more short story was required for the course, and Elizabeth dutifully turned it in. She had worked hard on it and thought it was the best of the three, though it was quite different from the first two. It was somewhat autobiographical, but it was the writing itself that she thought was stronger. However, she was resigned to Professor Doherty's unengaged commentary. Perhaps other professors in the program would discuss her work in greater depth.

She had read Professor Doherty's novel. The writing was clean, the novel balanced. Clearly he was a competent writer. Yet the novel itself was unmemorable. What did stick in her mind was a sex scene, which seemed quite self-conscious. The protagonist was on a beach with his girlfriend, making love for the first time, his initiation. One image, though, was striking: his orgasm like a silk scarf sliding out of his penis. Yet the woman was a cipher, with no feelings or awareness. She existed merely as a receptacle to provide him with an experience.

So it was with little anticipation that Elizabeth entered Professor Doherty's office for the last conference. She expected the same superficial comments, the same reserve. But Professor Doherty did not even address this last story. Instead, he said, "I have to tell you that you have not been accepted into the program."

Elizabeth looked blank.

"The subject matter of your stories is just not acceptable. No one can be expected to care about a female protagonist who casually has sex outside marriage. Or one who, unattractive woman that she is, allows herself to be exploited in a most brutal fashion. Your women have an unhealthy preoccupation with sex."

Elizabeth couldn't think what to say. She had always written in isolation and now felt that she needed the guidance of serious criticism. She had really wanted this program. She tried to get him to reconsider.

"If I submitted another story . . ." she began, but he cut her off.

"I'm sorry, but you just don't fit the program," he said with finality, and stood up.

There was nothing for her to do but leave.

~~~

For a long time, her confidence in herself was shaken, Elizabeth remembered now, looking back on the long vista of years. How different the world had become. Those born after the sixties simply had no conception of the world she had grown up in. Elizabeth smiled to think how shocked she was as a youngster, seeing Gone With the Wind *for the first time, when Rhett Butler turns to Scarlett and says, "Frankly, my dear, I don't give a damn." She remembered clearly when the ban on* Lady Chatterly's Lover *had been lifted. In the intervening years, she had read* A Room of One's Own *and* Three Guineas, *taken a*
~~~

women's studies course, read the radical feminists, led consciousness raising groups. Forty years ago she hadn't understood the context of Professor Doherty's criticism. A part of her had rebelled against his judgment, but still, she was a novice struggling to find her way. Although young, Dr. Doherty was a professor in a graduate writing program at a highly respected university.

Well, Elizabeth thought, she had eventually found her way and the world had changed, thank God. Three women were now on the Supreme Court. Medical schools and law schools filled with women. A few female CEOs made the news. Those stories she had submitted to Professor Doherty so long ago would make no sense to the young women of today, ambitious women who lived independently and claimed their own sexuality. Elizabeth felt a warm glow as she thought of her own modest contributions to this new world.

She made a cup of hot tea with milk and honey, raw local honey, and settled down on the comfortable sofa, remembering. So many years ago, but still vivid in her mind. The long mall, rising from the bronze steeds cavorting in the waters of the fountain, the spray sometimes shimmering with prismatic rainbows, the mall walks rising to the soaring, phallic tower, hallmark of the university. The clear bright light, an artist's light. In memory, she walked up the steps beside the fountain and paused to gaze up the long mall toward the tower, in her day the Main Building, etched against the sky in the brilliant light. Parallel sidewalks flanked the wide grassy mall where small groups of students sat in the warm sunshine. She chose the lefthand walk that led in front of white limestone buildings, one of which—Parlin Hall—housed the English Department. A line of live oak trees shaded the walk and the stone benches placed along it at regular intervals. A student intent on her book sat on one. Across the wide grassy interval, a similar walk shaded by live oaks also led past equally spaced buildings to the broad steps that ascended to the Main Building. In her imagination, she paused before she walked up the steps, as she had so often done as an undergraduate. She looked back at the sunny mall and the shady walks where, fresh from a philosophy class, a group of fellow students had often lingered long to debate the great questions. Nostalgia for that time of self-discovery and idealism crept over her. Once again in her mind's eye she gazed up at the inscription on the tower: Ye Shall Know the Truth and the Truth Shall Make You Free.

Athena, her fluffy gray cat, leapt up on the sofa, startling her, and curled up on her lap, softly purring. The setting sun, visible through the living room's west window, glowed golden in a cloudless sky. The faint tick of an old-fashioned clock at the far end of the room was barely audible, and the cup of tea felt warm in her hand. It was the quiet, reflective time of day.

But also the news hour. Elizabeth reached for the remote without unduly disturbing Athena and turned on the TV. For the first time in history, a woman was the candidate of a major party for the presidency of the United States.

The broadcast had already started, and it took Elizabeth a moment to get oriented. The screen was filled with an angry, gesticulating crowd, an overflow from a big convention center where the candidate of the other major party, a crude and wealthy womanizer, had been rabidly rousing his supporters.

Elizabeth gently stroked Athena, whose purring increased in volume, and sipped the sweet hot tea.

She gazed, puzzled, at the agitated, milling crowd who waved signs and shouted violent slogans, the camera panning across their combative faces.

Athena stretched, licked her paws, cleaned her face, then curled more tightly in Elizabeth's lap, purring faintly.

The camera zoomed in on a reporter at the scene who held a microphone close up to an irate man: what were his thoughts on the candidacy of the first woman ever to win the nomination of a major political party, a woman with an extensive resume of public service, including a major cabinet position?

The camera focused, even closer, on the man's scowling face. In the background, the massive crowd began chanting, "Lock her up, lock her up."

"She's nothing but a cun__," he got out before the television's censor bleeped him out.

Made in the USA
San Bernardino, CA
21 June 2018